DUST TO DUST

DECONSTRUCTION
BOOK ONE

By Rashad Freeman

Writing fiction has given me a chance to explore myself, my ambitions and my motivations in a deeper way. It's a therapeutic endeavor and in some ways, it's like taking a stroll through the cluttered forest of one's own mind and never coming out the other end. Wandering with no real purpose, picking up sticks or overturning stones, taking turns down long, dark paths and questioning everything from as many angles as possible. The more we strive to know, the more we realize how little we actually do.

While my writing is entertainment I hope some find more than that. I hope through my stories some challenge themselves to become more inquisitive and curious. I hope that my words stir more questions than answers and push toward the goal of self reflection. In the end, these aren't simply stories, but opportunities for a greater discussion or a look into what if. I hope you enjoy.

"Maybe it's always the end of the world. Maybe you're alive for a while, and then you realize you're going to die, and that's such an insane thing to comprehend, you look around for answers and the only answer is that the world must die with you." – Jess Walter

CHAPTER 1

TIP OF THE ICEBERG

I remember waking up that morning and thinking, *turn that shit off*. Alistair, my oldest son, had taken the liberty of flooding the house with some of his "dance music." It sounded more like cats being drowned while someone kicked over garbage cans in the background.

"Alistair!" I yelled. "Seriously?"

"What? It helps me get dressed."

"Too bad, turn it off now!"

Huffing, he thumbed through his Iphone, past his snapchat's and insta-whatevers and found the music app. He glanced up at me with all the teenage contempt he could muster, then reluctantly hit the pause button.

"You happy now?"

"No, but at least I don't have to commit a homicide at six AM."

He grinned and shrugged his shoulders. Then went back to rifling through his closet, to find the perfect t-shirt that broadcasted his aversion to all things government. Alistair was that kind of kid, the buzzword they loved to use was socially conscious. So, unlike most kids his age, he knew who was running for the state senate and I guess that qualified him as some kind of political critic.

He was sixteen going on thirty and had lived half of his life as an only child. I liked to think that explained some of his odd quirks, since he spent more time playing board games with me and my wife, than doing whatever kids did at that age. But the truth was, he was an old soul and I was more like his older brother than his father.

"I killed a snake last night," he said casually.

"What?"

"It was swimming in the pool. I think it was poisonous so..." He made the universal motion for death, swiping his index finger across his throat with a gagging sound.

"You feel better?"

"Meh, just letting you know...dangerous things are out there."

I laughed and headed into the hall. I could hear my wife up ahead waking up our two youngest, David and Charlie. They were eight and six respectively and the combination made for a ball of entertainment.

"I'm tired," Charlie moaned.

It was his daily argument before school. For reasons beyond me he could never get enough sleep and was all too eager to let everyone know it. He was a skinny kid, with a high-pitched voice and loose, curly hair. His drastic mood swings had earned him the name "Sour patch kid." You know, sour, sweet, gone.

"Don't forget to grab pork chops on the way home," Melinda instructed.

I nodded and stared at her for a few seconds with greedy eyes. Everything she said dripped with her Puerto Rican accent and it honestly gave flavor to a bunch of rather bland words.

"Say that again," I said.

"Say what?"

"Pork chops...it's sounds funny."

She smiled, half amused, half annoyed. "Shut up Randall."

I smacked her on the ass then headed into our room. I had exactly forty-five minutes to make it into the office and I was seriously slacking.

I paused for a few and stared up at the TV. Some news anchor was on, talking about extreme weather headed our way. They used that term far too frequently, since in Florida everything was extreme.

"If you keep an eye on the storm's track, you can see it's predicted to make landfall on the east coast as a category four. But, it could run into this warm weather pattern and possibly increase to a category five, making it the strongest storm to hit the east coast in recent history," the blonde-haired woman said with as much certainty as a kid explaining the Pythagorean theorem in front of the entire class. "We expect to see a lot of localized flooding and some very extreme weather, so those in evacuation zones A through C should start looking for higher ground. Don't wait, this is a massive system with the highest sustained wind speed we've ever seen. Damage from this storm will be off the charts."

I absolutely loathed people that could only speak in superlatives. The news was always trying to convince the world that death was around the corner. Be scared, do everything, do nothing, that was the message. How could anyone decipher the real crisis from the bullshit constantly flashing on the television.

It was early December and our weather was doing its normal crazy act. That meant it was forty-five degrees when I woke up. Sixty degrees when I headed to work. Ninety degrees when I went to lunch and seventy-eight degrees with rain on my way home. I didn't think the weather could get much more extreme than that.

I changed the channel as I pulled on my pants and laughed as the next anchor complained about our declining relations with Russia. It was simple in my eyes, we didn't like them, they didn't like us, but we both had big guns so the whole mutually assured destruction, kept the balance.

The news had me convinced that I wouldn't live to be a grandfather anyway. If it wasn't Russia it was North Korea and if it wasn't either one of them it was some idiot with a gun or gluten. Gluten might have been the scariest of them all.

"I'm leaving," Melinda said from the doorway.

Turning away from the TV, I glanced over at her and whistled. Her medium, ash-colored hair was slightly curled and fell just below her shoulders. She was leaning against the doorframe, beaming at me with her deep, brown eyes like she had a secret to tell, but needed to be convinced to tell it.

I walked over and gave her a kiss then gave Alistair a fist bump. "Don't do too much world changing today huh," I said.

Alistair laughed. "It's Friday...it's my day off."

Melinda leaned in and whispered, "Don't forget the PORK CHOPS."

Turning around, she giggled and headed out of the door. Alistair followed her as I finished getting David and Charlie ready for school. They groggily went through the motions, but eventually I was able to get them in the car and off to get their learning for the day.

After that I headed for downtown where I worked as an IT Risk Manager for some sleazy financial management company. It wasn't much, but it kept the lights on and allowed the kids to stay busy with sports and what not.

"You see the news this morning?" Steve asked as I walked into the break room.

He was a fair skinned blonde guy that liked the gym more than he liked women. When he wasn't working out he was busy spray tanning which meant every other week his skin had a bizarre orange haze.

"You talking about the shit with Russia?" I asked.

"No, not that," he said dismissively.

"The storm that's supposed to hit?" I guessed again.

"What? No. There was an earthquake in Brooksville."

I looked at him with a screwed-up face and laughed. One thing Florida was not known for was its earthquakes. I was certain Steve had heard wrong. Besides, I had a general idea of how earthquakes worked and I was certain we would've felt something being less than an hour away.

"Steve, you've had one too many steroids. I don't know what news you were watching this morning."

"I'm telling you man, I know what I saw."

Shrugging, I left him in the break room and headed for my desk. I had a pile of audit requests to go over and his misunderstanding of the news would have to wait.

"It's the end of the world Randall I'm telling you," he yelled after me with a laugh.

As if on cue a crackle of thunder erupted and giant globs of water splashed to the ground outside. I looked back at Steve one last time and gave him the middle finger.

Throughout the day, the general mood in the office was a bit bleak. People griping about how hectic the ride home would be in the rain and staring out of windows as the roads turned into small rivers. Any excuse to get out of work.

This was the norm. If it drizzled for longer than an hour the collecting rain became treacherous rapids that rendered motor vehicles useless. It wasn't out of place to see people skiing behind jacked-up trucks or paddling canoes down the road. Floridians had a unique perspective on what constituted a storm.

I was wrapping up my tenth audit report when a crowd of folk gathered around one of the TV's. They were all gasping and covering their mouths as if a suspense movie was playing. Annoyed, I stood up and looked to find out what all the fuss was about.

Hating myself, I gasped as well. The portly news anchor spoke erratically, constantly looking over his shoulder as the wind and rain whipped by. Debris sailed across the road behind him and street signs threatened to become missiles.

It looked like it was nighttime where he was, but it was a little past noon. His red raincoat was useless under the hail of water spears and his hand trembled as he held the microphone close to his mouth.

"Again, a tornado has touched down in Manhattan!" he yelled over the roar of the wind. "Several buildings have been damaged and...wait, we have a report of another..." the signal suddenly went out.

Just as his words died abruptly and people's mouths fell open, a series of three cacophonous booms rattled the walls inside of the office. The simultaneous flashes of lightning sent people rushing away from the windows as they cowered their heads in a frightful panic. The buzzing UV lights flickered and I could hear the UPS popping from the data center one floor below.

"Holy shit," Steve said and stopped beside me. "End of the world dude."

"Steve shut up."

"I know you don't give a shit, you've been waiting for this moment huh?"

I rolled my eyes and watched the wind push around the palm trees outside. Steve chuckled then flagged down Jason and Lou, two more audit managers that worked in the office.

"What do you think all this shit is about?" Lou asked.

He was a tall, lanky guy with red hair and a habit of getting shitfaced then showing up to work the next day like nothing happened. While he was well into his forties, he certainly partied like he was trying to get into a frat.

"It's Florida and it's raining," Jason replied.

He was a dark skin guy with slowly graying hair. He was barely into his thirties, but this job had a way of aging folk.

"Randall says he's got the bag ready to go," Steve added and shoved me on the arm.

"You gonna give me shit about it forever? Ain't nothing wrong with being prepared."

Jason laughed. "Your bug out bag huh? Had to give an emergency kit a cool name."

"Emergency kits don't go bang," I replied. "Besides, zombies are gonna happen. You'll regret you didn't listen to me."

They all shared a laugh at my expense, but my half-assed preparations were at least something. A hiking bag filled with the essentials: water, food rations, knives, a 9mm, ropes, flint rocks, flashlights etc. And a broom closet full of water and food survival buckets that would last for thirty years. I wouldn't call myself a

13

prepper, but I had a healthy suspicion about our government's ability to keep me safe.

"Don't listen to Randall, he's a poser," Lou laughed. "You ever been to the range with this idiot?"

"No, why?" Jason asked.

"Remember back when Eric came down to visit?"

"The military guy?"

"Yeah, he took us all shooting. Rambo here couldn't even load his own gun. Eric had to do it for him and when he finally did shoot, he couldn't hit a target from ten feet away."

I groaned. "That was a long time ago you asshole."

"You been since?"

I chuckled and shook my head from side to side. "Doesn't mean I won't be ready when the zombies come."

"You and this zombie shit," Steve replied. "And you don't think we had an earthquake in Brooksville?"

"Oh, we did," Jason hopped in. "First one in like forever. Couple of people died."

While Steve wasn't necessarily a source for sound information, Jason was normally reliable. So when he agreed I started to get a bit concerned.

"Hey guys," a voice suddenly called from behind us.

I turned to find Shannon Newlin, head of HR, standing a few feet away. She was rocking back and forth on her feet, certainly trying to disperse the weight that was focused on her tiny heels. Her upturned nose was all anyone ever needed to know about her, but with that she added a permanent scowl and shoddy, bleached blond hair.

"What's up Shannon?" I asked.

"Randall," she replied sharply. "Jason and Lou...and Steve," she finished.

There was a rumor going on around the office that Shannon and Steve had hooked up. Steve denied it, for obvious reasons and no one was going to question the most evil HR lady in history. So, it would have to remain unconfirmed.

"Emergency ops has reports of extreme thunderstorms," Shannon continued. "They're issuing a hurricane warning and evacuating flood areas. Needless to say, we're closing the office. Go home."

CHAPTER 2

THERE IS NO CALM
BEFORE THE STORM

As I drove down the flooded streets I started to truly appreciate my gas guzzling Suburban. While other cars had to look for alternative routes, I sloshed through the rising streams like a tank. I passed several disabled vehicles on the way and the increasing waves of emergency responders made me wonder if maybe Steve was onto something.

I pulled up to my house a little after three in the afternoon. Melinda had already picked up the kids and aside from the thunder and pounding rain it seemed like a normal day.

"They cancelled school early," Melinda said as I walked inside. "I need to log on and wrap up a few things."

Melinda was an operations manager for one of the big accounting firms. With a global workforce, even potential hurricanes didn't slow things down. So, working from home on her off time was kind of the norm.

"Just hurry up. Don't stay in there for four hours or we're gonna eat dinner without you."

Melinda chuckled then disappeared into the office. I headed into the kitchen and grabbed a bag of chips from the pantry.

"I heard there was an earthquake somewhere around here," Alistair said.

"Supposedly in Brooksville," I replied. "Is that what all of the cool kids are talking about these days?"

Alistair shrugged. "Where's Brooksville?"

"About an hour north of here. You hungry?"

"I am!" David yelled as he cleared the corner.

"When are you not?" Alistair jabbed. "Sooner or later you're gonna stop growing up and start growing out."

David was the middle child and like all middle children he was special. Unlike Alistair and Charlie, he had straight hair, which meant it was better than everyone else's. He constantly spent hours in the restroom styling and parting it just right.

He was big for his age and ever since the doctors had told him he'd be well over six foot four, he'd become intolerable. If you listened to him, he was already signed to an NBA team.

17

"All this sage wisdom Alistair. You're like a mixed Buddha with bad hair," I said in David's defense.

He smirked at me and mumbled something under his breath. Then, before I could say anything else a clap of thunder erupted so loud, I was certain I'd been hit.

"Holy shit!" Alistair shouted.

"Hey!"

"I'm sorry, but did you hear that? I mean like Holy shit!"

"Ahhh," Charlie yelled as he came running from his room.

His skinny frame looked comical as he rounded the corner at full speed. His eyes were wide and his face pale with fear. Without slowing down, he dove at me and wrapped his arms around my shoulders like a monkey.

"Calm down Charlie," I said and patted his back. "It's fine."

As if to make me a liar another rattling boom shook the walls and seemed to echo long after it was over. Melinda shrieked and then found her way to the kitchen with everyone else, like it was some kind of safe room.

"This storm is getting stupid," she complained.

"Welcome to Florida. You want a chip?"

"No, I want dinner. I actually wanted pork chops," she paused and smirked at me. "You know pork chops...those funny sounding things that I asked you to get this morning."

I frowned and shrugged my shoulders. "Yeah, I was kind of trying to not die on my way home. But we have chicken...you get these little hooligans and I'll start cooking."

Melinda raised an eyebrow. "I told you I had to wrap up a few things."

"That was before you ran out of the office afraid of a little lightning. Besides, the internet is gonna go down any minute."

"Fine, but hurry up. David, Charlie, let's go clean your room. Alistair, you definitely need to clean yours and clean your bathroom."

"Yeah," I added. "Looks like a homeless man committed suicide in there."

"You guys are ruining my life," he said with a sarcastic grin then flailed his arms and took off around the corner.

"That's your child," Melinda chuckled.

"So you've told me."

I ran into my room and changed into some gym clothes then started doing my best impression of Masterchef. It had become a well-known fact around the house that I was serious about my cooking. I'd even bought a few books to grow my blossoming chef skills. Sooner or later I was gonna be Michelin quality, although I didn't really know what that meant.

I opened the refrigerator and grabbed a few chicken breasts. I greased a pan and turned the oven to bake at 375. As I prepared to shove the chicken inside, the digital pad went blank and every light in the house went out.

"Fuck!" I grumbled. "Power's off."

I went to the windows and twisted all of the blinds open. The darkening sky outside offered little illumination so I started searching for flashlights. In the back of my mind I thought of my survival bag and how I might actually get to use it. Power outage, flat tire, hell as far as I was concerned, a bee sting was reason enough to take out the go bag.

Scouring the house, I cursed my need for clutter. Nothing had its own spot and I tended to toss things wherever I was standing at the moment I no longer needed them. I paid for that laziness in times like these.

I finally found a dusty, red flashlight under the kitchen counter and clicked it on. The light flickered and then shut off. I banged my hand against the case several times, but that did nothing to solve my lighting issues.

"Time for the bag," I grumbled to myself with a smile.

Feeling my way through the darker parts of the house, I made it to the broom closet. Sitting on the floor was my orange hiking bag that was stuffed full of goodies. I opened it up and grabbed one of my LED flashlights and depressed the clicker. Nothing. I pressed it again and then let out an angry groan and raised my arm to chuck the thing across the house.

"What are you doing?" Melinda asked. She was standing behind me holding a candle.

"Um, I... you know, it's an emergency, I need the bug out bag."

She sighed and shook her head. "Go to *McDonalds*...the kids are starving."

"Yes ma'am. Did you want me to grab you something?"

"No, I'll figure it out later. Just bring them something back."

Nodding, I tossed my bag back into the closet and closed the door. I slipped on my sandals then grabbed the keys and headed outside. The rain had slowed to a pathetic drizzle and the lightning had decided to torment some other part of the state. It was starting to look like our little storm had run out of steam. In the two minutes since I had opened the blinds the sky had done a one-eighty. Welcome to Florida.

With the key fob in my hand, I pressed the unlock button, but nothing happened. *I knew I should've changed those damn batteries a month ago.* They had been working on and off for the last few weeks and it figured now would be the time they completely die.

Like a cave man, I walked over to the door and put my key into the lock. It took me a few times to get it to fit, but eventually I was able to gain entry without the use of technology.

Opening the door, I hopped inside of my Suburban and shook off the rain droplets that had collected on my head. I laughed as the water in the road had already begun to recede and the sky seemed to be brightening a bit.

With a twist of the key into the ignition, I waited for the satisfying engine grumble, that I had come to expect like I was one of Pavlov's dogs. When nothing happened, I tried again and again then banged my fists on the steering wheel in desperation. The day was starting to mount a serious war of bullshit and I was on the losing end.

"Can't get it to start huh?" Jake, my neighbor, shouted from his lawn.

He was an older guy from New York. He normally came down in the winter and hosted poker games on the weekend. I was pretty sure he was retired, but I never really saw much of him during the day.

Grunting, I stepped outside and stretched my legs. "What the hell is going on?" I asked.

"Can't get mine to start either. Crazy storm we got going on here," Jake replied and scratched his head.

I looked up at the sky and laughed a bit. "Yeah, it's crazy. Crazy like not there."

"Hey what's going on Randall?" a voice called from behind me.

I turned and found Mike and Greg, my other neighbors heading over. Mike was a general contractor and Greg was an insurance agent. They were a little bit older than me, but Mike and I had kids around the same age and Greg was his friend.

"My trucks broken I guess. Dead battery or something," I replied."

"Nah," Mike said with certainty. "Not a car on the block is working. Greg says it's some kind of EMP."

"What!? Greg, you went straight to end of the world huh? That's supposed to be my thing."

"Come on Randall, what else would explain a bunch of cars not working? You think everyone got the same faulty battery?"

"No clue...but this day is just one big L."

"Hell yeah," Mike laughed. "Earthquakes in Brooksville, tornadoes in New York. It sounds like a damn movie."

Jake looked like he wanted to add something, but before he could, the sky opened up and unleashed enough water to drown a fish. A series of flashes made the hair on my arms stand on end and the accompanying raucous nearly made me piss myself.

Without another word, we all took of sprinting for our respective homes. I shuffled up the steps and bolted inside in a hurry. I was accustomed to the erratic weather, but lightning was one thing all Floridians respected.

"I thought you were getting food," Alistair said as I nearly ran him over.

"Yeah...I was. But it looks like we'll be eating something here. Time to make sandwiches."

I headed into the kitchen and grabbed a loaf of bread. Ignoring Alistair's protests, I started prepping my little workstation like I was a Subway employee.

"You're back already?" Melinda asked as she came out of the bedroom. "The phones aren't working

"What phones?"

"None of the phones. The house phone, my cell phone...none of the phones."

"What the hell is going on? It's the damn Russians, they fuck up everything," I laughed.

"Where's the food? You said you'd go and get food."

"Well it looks like the cars aren't working either."

Melinda frowned and shook her head from side to side. "Randall that's not funny."

"I'm not laughing. Nobody's car is working. I talked to Mike and Greg outside. They said the whole block is the same."

"Okay now I'm getting scared," Melinda said seriously.

I reached into my pocket and pulled out my cell phone. The screen was black and no matter what buttons I pressed, I couldn't get anything to work. I immediately thought of Alistair and how his world must be crumbling to dust.

"You try charging the phone?"

Melinda didn't respond. She was staring off into nothing with a blank look on her face. She was nervous and a little voice inside of me said she had every right to be.

"Melinda," I called again. "Did you try charging it?"

"Charging what?"

"The phone."

"It was on the charger. It doesn't work Randall...nothing freaking works."

The weather outside picked up and I could now hear the wind whipping down the street and shuddering the windows. The front door creaked softly as the intense gusts pushed it back and forth in its pocket. It sounded like boulders were being thrown around in the middle of the road.

"Dad, are we gonna die?" David suddenly asked.

"What? No, we're not gonna die. Everything is gonna be fine. Look I'm gonna make sandwiches then we're gonna eat and go to bed. Tomorrow I'm sure they'll have all of this sorted out and then we can go and get some real food."

One more thundering clap right outside of the door punctuated my last word. Sighing, I looked around and stared outside at the sideways rain. It was just a storm, I told myself. It was always **just** a storm.

CHAPTER 3

PASSING THE TIME

I awoke the next morning to a bright sunny sky. It was a little past nine and the only evidence that we'd had any inclement weather was a few upturned palm trees. Like I said, it was just a storm.

Crossing my fingers, I walked to the wall and flipped on the light switch. No luck. I was expecting that, but hope dies hard.

"Power still off?" Melinda asked as she sat up and shrugged off the blankets.

"Yep...thank God it's not hot anymore."

"It'll start getting hot pretty soon. Have you checked your phone?"

"No... I think I heard Greg and Mike outside though. I'm gonna head out and see if they know anything."

After brushing my teeth and grabbing a t-shirt, I headed outside. Mike, Greg and a few of the other neighborhood guys, whose names I didn't know, were circled on the sidewalk, talking with big hand motions.

"What's up guys?" I said as I approached.

"Hey what's up Randall? This is Bobby and Trent, they stay around the corner."

"Nice to meet you," I said and shook both of their hands.

"So Trent is like an amateur meteorologist. Tell him what you told us," Mike said with a smile.

"Definitely an EMP. Not a doubt in my mind."

"What? That's like nuclear attack and shit," I retorted. "Why does everyone want to blame a damn EMP?"

"Nuclear attack is what everyone knows about. That's just what's popular. Lightning storms can cause EMP's too. And the storm we just had was definitely big enough for that."

"Okay, so what now? I mean my phones off, my car doesn't work, there's no power in the house. I'm over here regretting that I never built a bunker."

"It's a problem, I definitely don't have all of the answers. I'm sure Emergency responders are working on it though. And the power company should already be out replacing transformers. It's probably best to just stay at your house until they get some of the grid back up and running."

I looked at Trent skeptically then turned to Mike for reassurance. I didn't know the guy and he was spouting off things like he worked for the government. It's always like that, people pop their heads out, swearing they're experts.

"Trent used to work for FEMA, he's seen a lot of shit," Mike added as if he could read my mind.

"Yeah, this ain't that bad," Trent went on, letting his bravado get the best of him. "Katrina, now that was some shit. Dead bodies floating down the road, black guys with TV's in one hand and shotguns in the other," he paused and gave me a tentative look.

I guess as the resident black guy it was up to me to judge the level of racism anytime someone brought up color. I really didn't care, Trent seemed like one of those guys that watched too much Discovery channel and thought he was Bear Grylls.

"So how do we fix our cars?" Mike asked, breaking the awkward silence.

"Well, all small electronics are gonna need repair. No way of getting around that, insurance should cover most if not all damages though."

"Your advice is to stay home and wait for someone to come knocking? What about food? What about water?" I asked.

"I'm sure someone will be out today. Wouldn't shock me if you were watching your favorite porno in the living room by lunch time."

"Who the hell watches porno in the afternoon?" his friend, Bobby laughed.

"Well, you know what I mean."

"Told you it was an EMP," Greg bragged. "I just knew it was."

I shook my head and cut my eyes. Greg was such a tool. Him and Mike were like the hype men for Trent and as far as I could tell Trent was just making shit up.

"It's this uppity lifestyle," Bobby suddenly said.

"What?"

"I mean the world could end and what the hell would we know behind our gates. It's just us and the damn bay. A bunch of stuck up house wives..."

"And house husbands," I cut in and shot a glance at Trent.

"Yeah...yeah, just assholes that wanted to live near the ocean. Now we sit back here and have no clue what's going on."

He was right and brought up something I hadn't even considered. The neighborhood backed up against the Tampa Bay. And to the front were imposing wrought, iron gates that were electronically controlled and required an access badge to open. The road that led up to them was narrow and barricaded on both sides by the lagoon.

It was a mile to the front of the neighborhood and the Welcome Center, which was tucked behind a type of tropical oasis. It would be another mile until you made it to the nearest business, a grocery store and brand new business park with a couple of boutique shops.

We were secluded enough that information would take a while to reach us. It was as close to being away from the world as you could come, while still being in the middle of everything.

29

"I'm gonna head back in, see what I can find for breakfast. Mike, let me know if you hear anything else," I said as I grew tired of the speculation game.

"Yeah, of course," Mike replied.

I said my goodbyes and headed back inside to a pack of hungry kids and a nervous wife. They were all sitting at the kitchen table, pondering their choices of cereal. This was where it started, this was where social order of life slowly deconstructed and we let our animal instincts take over. All at the kitchen table.

"Well?" Melinda asked.

"Some guy says it's an EMP from the lightning storm. What the hell does he know though? Either way, nothing is working right now, so we just sit it out til the power guys get out here."

"And what about the truck?"

"Still broken. Did you try your car?" I asked.

"No, you said no one's car was working. Why would I need to try mine?"

I felt a little bit of optimism rise in my chest and I snatched her keys from the wall. Without another word, I ran into the garage and jumped inside of her Toyota.

Placing my foot on the brake, I pressed the start button and was greeted with the same lifeless silence as my truck outside. "Damn it!" I snapped.

"Did you actually think it was gonna work?" Alistair laughed from the door.

"Shut up," I replied and closed the car. "It was worth a shot."

30

"My phone isn't working," he groaned as I passed him and went back inside.

"You survived longer than I thought you would. Nobody's phone is working. Go read a book."

Alistair grunted then went to his room and closed the door. *The life of a sixteen-year-old was such a rough existence.* If he didn't start a full-on mutiny in the next hour, I'd be shocked.

"Your car's not working either," I told Melinda.

"Well duh. So, what are you going to do?"

"What can I do? Cars are broken, phones are broken. Someone needs to fix it all."

"And what, you think the fix-it fairy is on her way out here?"

I laughed. "Something like that. Once the power company gets the phones working we can call someone out about the car and go from there. Don't be such a sarcastic ass."

"Uh huh," she replied and clicked her teeth. "Pork chops."

I smirked. The rest of the day we passed the time playing board games or hide and seek throughout the house. David and Charlie were having the time of their lives and even Alistair seemed to find some kind of joy in it.

It was funny how simple life could be. You take away the phones and televisions...all of the distractions and suddenly things became much less complicated.

Before I knew it, the sun had fallen and we'd wasted the day away pretending to be kids again. Thanks to mother nature, every appointment or possible errand was not even a thought and we burned the day away the way God probably intended.

CHAPTER 4

OUT AND ABOUT

As Monday morning neared the mood around the neighborhood had drastically changed. It was winter break for the kids, but that didn't mean we got off that easy.

No one had come out. No one's power had been restored. And as far as I knew, no one had heard from anyone outside of our neighborhood or attempted to venture out.

This was starting to turn into a bad movie, where the world ended, but no one told the residents of Island Bay. I felt like we'd waited long enough and the help that Trent said was coming was nothing more than a pipe dream.

"You still think emergency responders are on the way?" I asked Mike as we were sitting around on my porch watching the sun come up.

"Mike likes to try and be an optimist," his wife, Jennifer replied.

Jennifer was a nurse. She was an entire head taller than Mike with jet-black hair and olive skin. It didn't take much to picture her roaming the Amazon or fighting jaguars for the last piece of anaconda meat. But instead, she wore glasses and read books.

"I just think Mike's in love...it's okay I get it," I said with a laugh.

"Oh, is someone jealous?" Mike retorted.

"He gets that way," Melinda added. "He didn't want to share his toys when he was little either."

"Okay, this isn't beat up on Randall day."

Everyone laughed and took a collective sigh. I could sense the stress and while some hid it more than others, we all had the same fear buried deep down inside. The world was ending, something terrible had happened and we just didn't know it yet.

"How are the kids?" Melinda turned to Jennifer and asked.

"Not a fan of the dark, but they've taken over our bed so I guess they're managing. They're in there now hanging out with my dad. He came down for the weekend and now he's stuck, might as well put him to work."

They had two sons about the same age as David and Charlie. They played together every now and then and went to the same school. That practically made us best friends or at least as far as our children were concerned.

"How are yours doing?" Jennifer asked.

"They're loving it. Hide and seek for hours." Melinda laughed for a minute then cleared her throat. "Someone really needs to do something. It's been like three days," she said in a serious tone.

"Yeah, I don't know about you guys, but we're running out of stuff. Mike, why don't you and Randall walk up to the grocery store."

Mike groaned. He looked at me and drastically rolled his eyes then kicked his feet up and leaned back in his chair.

"The grocery store babe? That's like...that's like a long way away. I'm sure someone will be out here. I mean if any other neighborhoods are like ours, they're probably slammed."

Jennifer slapped Mike's legs down. "This isn't funny. We need something to drink and some more food that you don't have to cook. You could probably just take a shopping cart from up there and grab one of those charcoal grills out front of Ace."

Jennifer was getting carried away with her planning and I could see in Melinda's eyes she was about to join the crazy train. Chances were, we'd see the power company in a few hours and this would be something we all laughed about in a few weeks.

"Hold up now, we can't walk a grill back here," I said, choosing to throw my support behind Mike.

"Yeah, this whole idea is stupid." Mike added.

"Well your kids are gonna starve. There's nothing to eat here and barely anything to drink. And this morning the water stopped working," Jennifer snapped and shook her finger at Mike.

"What!" I was shocked to hear that. "Your water isn't working? I'll be right back."

I quickly ran inside and turned the handle to the nearest faucet. A steady stream of water shot out and I breathed a sigh of relief... short-lived relief.

Suddenly, the faucet started to sputter and the water spat out in uneven intervals. Then the last drop fell and there was nothing. I turned the handle on and off several times, cursing my crappy luck. Things were starting to get serious.

"Water is out," I announced as I headed back onto the porch with my head slumped. "Go get your shoes Mike. We're going to the store."

Jennifer clapped her hands together and Mike groaned. I shrugged and held my hands up. I didn't know what he wanted me to do, but our status had just taken a nose dive. It was time to get out and find out just what the hell was going on.

A few minutes later Mike reappeared, wearing a pair of sneakers and a baseball cap. He had his sons book bag strapped on his shoulders and his wallet clutched in his right hand.

"What are you doing?" Jennifer asked.

"Am I supposed to carry your crap in my hands?"

"Fine, just make sure you bring his bag back."

"Yes ma'am," Mike retorted. "Randall, you ready to go?"

"Just waiting on you," I replied.

I gave Melinda a kiss then headed down the steps to the sidewalk. Mike followed after me and together we started our two-mile journey.

"Where's my kiss?" Jennifer yelled after him.

"Ugh," he grunted then turned around.

Running back up the porch, he gave Jennifer a quick peck on the cheek. "You happy now?"

"Yes, actually I am. Stay safe out there."

Mike laughed. "What's the worst that can happen? We're just two well equipped guys going grocery shopping."

CHAPTER 5

GROCERY SHOPPING

The hefty gate at the front of the neighborhood was slammed shut. The chain that pulled it open and closed hadn't moved in a few days and was already collecting rust from the downpour days before. It felt like an ominous sign to me, but Mike didn't even seem to notice.

The guard tower at the front lay dormant. The doors were bolted shut and the windows had been boarded up. That however, had little to do with the storm. A few weeks earlier the homeowner's association decided to fire all of the guards. Now they were using some call center to grant visitor access and the general response from the community was less than pleased.

Luckily, the gate that blocked the sidewalk didn't use any kind of electronics or outsourced workforce. It had a keypad lock on it and after punching in a few digits we swung it open and headed out.

The water gently splashed onto the rocks of the lagoon as the wind picked up a bit. It wasn't storm weather, just the normal breeze that came unimpeded from the gulf. It was eerie now, but one of the main reasons we had chosen this neighborhood.

"It's peaceful out," Mike said more to himself. "Kinda like a vacation, I like vacations."

I nodded, even if the abandoned look gave me a bad feeling in the pit of my stomach. The lagoons were always full of boats going or coming. Canoes and paddle boarding was an everyday thing out here. The rippling water looked strange without some watercraft cresting through its surface. He was right though, it was peaceful out.

"So, we gonna steal a cart?" I asked.

"Yeah...I brought the bag to hide the liquor bottles."

"Fucking alcoholic."

"You try and deal with my two for a week and see if you don't develop an addiction."

I laughed and sped up a bit. "Come on, I wanna get there and get back home."

"What's the rush?"

"I don't know. I just have a funny feeling about all of this. Don't want to leave Melinda and the kids alone for too long."

"It's nothing man. You worry too much."

"You don't worry enough."

After about ten minutes we made it out of the neighborhood and headed down the back road to the grocery store. Most of the surrounding area was undeveloped and roads twisted through thick forests and wetlands. Small animals, or at least what I imagined to be small animals scurried through the dense vegetation beside us. Mike jumped a couple of times, but tried to play it off.

"It's weird," I started.

"What?"

"I haven't seen another person. It's like a ghost town around here."

"Well nobody's car works and people are lazy as hell. If it wasn't for your big mouth I sure as hell wouldn't be walking to the grocery store, but now that I am, I'm gonna make it worth my while," he said and tapped his sons book bag.

I frowned at him then continued on our way. As we walked the cool temperature started to turn muggy and hot. Florida hadn't surrendered to winter yet and was throwing one hell of a fit. Groaning, I wiped sweat from my face and used my shorts as a towel. They'd collected just about enough body fluid to be wrung out. The humidity in Florida had a way of making everything gross.

With my head slumped, I lazily trotted down the sidewalk. I let my feet coast on autopilot and started to compile a shopping list in my head. I knew water was a must, but I needed to think food. With no electricity, our choices for meals were severely limited and even if Trent was right, there was no telling when the power companies would make it to us.

"Shit!" Mike suddenly jumped.

I looked up and paused. A scraggily man in jeans and a flannel shirt was running towards us. He had two plastic bags clutched in his hands with snack cakes tumbling out of the top. Sweat was pouring down his scruffy face and his eyes were wild and bloodshot.

I moved over to the side and he rushed past us and kept going. Mike stared after him for a moment then turned to me and grinned.

"See, people are still alive man."

I laughed and kept walking. I wanted to get back home as soon as I could. With every step we took, I felt like I should turn back, like I was getting further and further away the moment that they needed me.

Every so often I looked over my shoulder. I wasn't sure why that guy was running or what he was running from, but he didn't seem too stable. I imagined him running back toward us and attacking Mike or trying to stab me. You could never be too careful.

Rounding the corner, we made it to the shopping plaza and stopped. Mike gasped and I felt the bottom of my stomach fall out. I'd been fighting a funny feeling the entire walk, but now I had a real reason to be worried.

People were running in and out of the stores, holding as much as they could carry in their arms. Some were scuffling over grocery items in the middle of the parking lot. Others were scavenging what people dropped as they hurried to loot other businesses.

The windows to the grocery store were broken and glass shards covered the walkway. The salon next door was on fire and trails of blood told stories of even darker crimes. Things like this, I'd only ever seen on the news.

"What the fuck?" Mike mumbled. "What the fuck."

"I had a feeling, I mean not like this, but I had a feeling it was gonna get bad."

Mike shot me a sideways glance then took a deep, thoughtful breath. "What do you want to do?"

"We're here now."

"You think it's safe?"

"I don't know, but we're gonna need food and water. Especially now, if we don't pick up some things they won't be here later. Let's go in, stick together and be quick."

Mike nodded and we moved toward the broken doors of the grocery store. I grabbed an empty shopping cart on the way in then headed straight for the water. Only a few bottles were left, but we quickly grabbed them then headed to the soft drinks.

"This is nuts," Mike continued to mumble. "It shouldn't be like this, there should be cops or something."

People were all over the store. It was a free for all and the crazed looks from everybody we passed told me it was gonna get ugly in here soon. Even the store employees had abandoned their posts and were grabbing as much as they could carry. At that point, the world wasn't ending, but everyone in earshot seemed to think it was.

As we turned the corner down another aisle, we almost crashed into three guys that were huddled together whispering in hushed voices. They froze when we appeared then gave us dirty looks and found another place to hold their meeting.

"What the hell do you think that was about?" Mike asked wearily.

"No clue, but I don't think it was something good. Let's hurry the hell up."

We quickly tried to get anything that could be eaten on the fly. Canned foods, bags of chips, peanuts even some lunch meat that we decided would go first. Mixed in with that were things like soap and rubbing alcohol and gauze. I was sure we'd missed some critical items, but we hadn't come to the store expecting Armageddon.

"I think this is enough," I said as Mike tossed another bag of charcoal into the cart.

We planned to grab one of those grills Jennifer asked about on our way back home. We weren't gonna tell her, but it was actually a good idea.

Mike nodded and we pushed the cart over the broken glass and started down the sidewalk. Stopping by Ace, we crammed a small grill on top of everything else then tried to hurry away, avoiding prying eyes.

"That wasn't so bad," Mike said.

"Yeah, I think we made it out before the crazy hit."

"Hey slow down!" a voice called from behind us.

I snapped my head around fast enough to give me a slight dizzy spell. Trotting behind us were the three guys we'd almost ran into earlier in the store. If possible they looked even shadier and I felt the rush of adrenaline that came with fight or flight.

"You guys made out in there huh?" the closest one asked.

He was skinny and lanky with dirty jeans and a frayed gray t-shirt. His buzzed, black hair was riddled with patches, like he'd pissed the barber off and he sported a gaudy, gold watch, that I was willing to bet hadn't belonged to him a day earlier.

"What's up?" Mike replied in a bold voice.

"What's up...what's up is you took all the Goddamn water," another one of the guys said.

He was a heftier fellow with long, dingy blonde hair. He was wearing cargo shorts and a green army jacket that was a bit too small.

Behind him, the last guy stepped forward to make sure we gave him the respect he was due. He was the shortest of them all and his gut was hanging out from under his tiny, gray shirt. He had a trucker hat on and a thick, brown beard with cookie crumbs stuck in it.

"Yeah," he said, backing up his friend. "You took the all the damn water and didn't leave any for us. So, we want your cart."

CHAPTER 6

THE BEGINNING OF THE

END

"Fuck off!" Mike said angrily and tightened his grip on the shopping cart.

Patches growled and jumped forward. I put my hands out and gave him a gentle nudge backwards then stepped in between him and the cart.

"Hey, calm down," I said.

"You calm down," Patches shot back. "You can't just take shit and not share. You didn't leave any water for anyone else."

"And you think you can just take all of our stuff. Over my dead body. Go back to the meth house," Mike continued his verbal assault.

Curly and Moe were still deciding how far they wanted to push this strong-arm snatch job. From what I could tell, Patches was the only real threat and he seemed hell bent on robbing us of everything.

"How about we split the water? There's enough to go around," I proposed.

Guys like that needed to feel like they got a win and I was trying to avoid some kind of street brawl. Without phones or police, things would probably get out of hand quickly. He looked like he was considering my offer, until Mike had to open his big mouth.

"Fuck that. We're not splitting shit. This is ours, you want some water find another store or head to a damn water fountain."

"Your friend's got a big mouth on him," Patches spat.

"Tell me about it."

"If he doesn't watch it someone is gonna close it for him...permanently."

Mike scoffed. "We don't have time for this. Randall let's go."

He wheeled the cart around and started to push it down the sidewalk. Patches suddenly lunged forward and shoved me aside. He grabbed Mike by the shoulder and pulled him back.

"You're not going anywhere with that cart."

Mike turned around and swung wildly. His misplaced punch caught Patches in the side of the neck as he continued to sail forward and almost fell.

Patches stumbled backward a few feet then recovered. He grabbed Mike by the shoulders then slung him to the ground. After that, it was on.

Curley and Moe decided I'd be the object of their aggression. The bigger one grabbed me while the fat runt buried his fist into my stomach. I coughed and collapsed forward on all fours.

My lungs burned as they prayed for air and I found myself back on a grade school playground, wishing I'd stay in those damn karate classes. I was too old to be getting my ass kicked now and I be damned if these two douche bags were the gonna be the ones to do it.

I took a deep breath and thought, *fuck it*. Air finally found its way into my chest just in time for me to recognize the foot that was surging toward my head. I slipped to the side just as it sailed by.

Pissed off, I jumped to my feet and dove at the chubby bastard that had just tried to make a field goal with my face. We collided like a car crash and slammed into the concrete. On my way down I caught a glimpse of Mike rolling across the ground with Patches.

"What the hell are yall doing?" the bigger one yelled.

All of a sudden, he didn't seem as convicted as his counterparts. He stood over me as I kneed and jabbed at his buddy, doing my best to replicate some moves I'd seen in a UFC fight.

"Come on guys, let's just go," he continued to plead.

I delivered another uppercut to his chubby friend and he gasped for air like a fish. I'd just dispatched a guy that probably spent his life playing Minecraft and eating flaming hot Cheetos. As belittling as that should've felt, I felt like I'd conquered the world.

A few feet away, Mike and Patches were really going at it. Both were bleeding and yelling obscenities with every swing they took. My little skirmish paled in comparison.

Mike shoved his elbow into Patches pelvis then kicked his leg out, finding a home in his tibia. With a howl, Patches staggered backward then let out an inhuman roar.

I could see the fear cultivating in Mike's eyes. This had gone from a friendly scuffle to a battle of life and death. Mike was ill-equipped and Patches was looking like he'd just decided to wake up.

Still screaming at the top of his lungs, Patches charged Mike and they went flying into a row of hedges. In a twisted web of legs and arms, they rolled through the mulch exchanging blows and verbal insults.

I lost view of them partially as they tumbled further into the dense leaves. I could hear Mike shouting like a mad man and then something exploded like a plate being dropped on a marble floor.

Everything stopped. Curly and Moe froze as their mouths dropped in shock. I stood there wild eyed with a million thoughts rushing through my head. It wasn't until I heard Mike groan and Patches stood up that I regained some mobility.

I ran to the bushes, where Mike was laying on his back with his legs sprawled out in the grass. His hand was pressed tightly against

48

the side of his stomach, desperately trying to staunch the flow of blood that had already drenched his t-shirt.

"What the hell did you do?" the heftier man asked, his voice trembling in panic. "What the hell?"

Patches was standing a few feet away with a small pistol in his hand. A thin tail of smoke swirled from the barrel and I could see the shock painted all over his face.

"I... I, I didn't mean to. It...it just went off," he stuttered.

"Let's get out of here," the chubbier man declared.

"Randall," Mike moaned and reached out to me.

I grabbed his hand and knelt beside him. "Somebody help, somebody help me!" I screamed, every word dripping with trepidation.

"I didn't mean to...I'm sorry," Patches pleaded to deaf ears.

He stuffed the pistol back into his pants then looked around. His two anxious friends had already started retreating. With one last glance, they tore off the way they came.

Mike's face was pale and his breathing seemed difficult. His eyes were hazy, but I could see the despair in them. He had the look of a man that had seen death face on and had crumbled beneath the morbid gaze.

I'd never seen anyone injured like that before. No one that had gone from alive and vibrant to clinging to life in a snap. I'd seen plenty of scary movies, twisted, demented tales, but this was what pure horror looked like. Only when faced with our mortality could we ever truly embrace real, palpable fear.

"I don't want to die," Mike said in an almost childish voice.

His words snapped me out of my daze and my brain started working in overload.

"You're not gonna die Mike," I replied.

I jumped up and ran to the cart that had thankfully been left by the band of murdering assholes. I rummaged around until I found the package of gauze and some disinfectant.

"Don't you fucking leave me!" Mike yelled after me.

I took his belligerence as a good sign and felt that just maybe he'd make it out of this. "Nobody is leaving you. I'm gonna fix you up crybaby."

Honestly, I had no clue what I was doing, but common sense told me I need to clean it and try and stop the bleeding. Both of those goals ended in failure.

"Hold still," I instructed as I poured the disinfectant over his wound.

As soon as the liquid hit him he let out a wail that damn near busted my eardrums. He reeled and squirmed in pain, kicking up mulch and other debris that landed on top of him.

With a handful of gauze, I pressed down on the little hole in his side. The white mesh quickly turned red and was rendered useless by the amount of blood oozing from him. I grabbed another box and ripped it open then stuffed the gauze on top of the old one.

"Fuck!" Mike yelled in agony.

I tried to hold him down, but he was throwing a fit squirming and twisting on the ground. More blood gushed from his wound and I knew if he didn't get help quickly he was going to die.

"Come on man, we've gotta get you home. Those chicks across the street are nurses or something."

Mike grunted and I took that as agreement. I grabbed his free hand and pulled him into a sitting position. I looked back at the cart and figured I could cram him in there if I moved the grill to the bottom shelf.

I left him there and moved a few things around to make room. Once I had a little pocket that I thought he could fit in I wheeled the cart over and started to pull him up.

"I'm cold man," he said as I grabbed his hand.

He shifted a bit to the side and I could see the puddle of blood that had been pouring from the hole in his torso. The entire back of his shirt was stained with the deepest, darkest shade of blood I'd ever seen. It was almost black.

"What?" Mike asked as my extended pause alarmed him.

"No... nothing. You're gonna be fine man."

I hoisted him into my arms and sat him into the cart as gently as I could. He groaned and cursed, but finally settled in. It looked uncomfortable being crunched up between jugs of water and canned foods, but we had little choice.

"You're gonna be okay Mike, just hold on," I told him. With trembling hands, I grabbed the buggy and started to push it toward home.

51

CHAPTER 7

THE BEARER OF BAD

NEWS

It was a little past midday and the warm muggy air had only gotten worse. Pushing the cart full of supplies and Mike had become quite a chore and I was sweating enough that I worried about dropping dead from dehydration.

"You okay up there Mike?" I asked after a solid five minutes of silence.

"Yarghh, yeah!" he garbled out.

His head was slumped back on a roll of paper towels and his legs were dangling out of the cart like spaghetti noodles. We were maybe half way home and I was praying that help would be waiting once I got there.

"Stay awake Mike," I ordered.

He was slipping in and out of consciousness and it was really starting to scare me. Whether the gauze was working or he'd run out of blood, his wound had stopped bleeding. But now his condition had taken a nose dive and I started trying to come to terms with the idea that I might have to tell his wife that he'd died.

Mike's face was peppered with beads of sweat. His lips had turned a light shade of blue and he was constantly mumbling under his breath in gibberish.

I pushed the cart as fast as I could, even running a bit with it when the sidewalk was smooth enough not to jolt him about. I could see the gates to our neighborhood coming up and I felt the slimmest of hope that Mike might make it out okay.

The sun beamed above me and every trace of clouds had been burned away. My forearms ached and the little squeaking wheels of the cart were driving me mad. My legs felt like lead and wobbled sporadically with every step I took, but I kept pushing, Mike needed me to keep pushing.

"You still with me buddy?" I asked as I reached the gate and started to punch in the code. "Mike?"

There was no answer. I took a deep breath and swallowed, trying to prolong the time before I turned around and saw what I already knew. This was Schrodinger's cat taken to a whole new level and I was willing to stand in limbo forever than be the one to open that box.

"Mike," I said and the crackle in my voice shocked me. "Answer me man."

With a heavy heart, I turned around. Pain stabbed me like needles as I stared at Mike's lifeless face and I felt a rush of emotions that I couldn't comprehend.

His eyes were dull and cloudy. His mouth hung open, his blue lips dry and cracked. It was obvious he'd taken his last breath, but I still wasn't ready to accept it.

"Mike!" I yelled. "Mike get up!"

I grabbed him by the shoulders and shook him vigorously. His head bounced back and forth and I shivered from the morbidity I felt. The sting of tears down my face was like a slap that brought me crashing to my knees.

This was someone's husband, someone's father. How was I gonna explain to Jennifer that Mike had been killed over a jug of water? How could I explain to his sons that their father was never coming back?

"Oh my God," I wailed.

With my face buried in my sweaty, bloodstained hands, I cried. I cried until the tears ran dry and my head beat like a drum. I cried until there was nothing left for me, but action. I cried until I had no choice, but to face reality and put one foot in front of the next. I cried for Mike, but more importantly, I cried for what his absence would mean for those that were left behind.

Mike and I were casual friends at best, but he loved his kids. He loved his wife and somehow, I felt responsible for stealing him from them. It was wrong that his last moments were spent with a man he only kind of knew. It was wrong that his sons would have to bury him long before he could ever teach them to shave, before he could teach them to be men themselves.

It was my fault we were even at the store. My idea to take all of the water. I hadn't pulled the trigger that killed Mike. But I'd put him there in front of the bullet.

I don't know how long I sat on the ground next to the cart that carried Mike's body, but at some point, a gentle rumble in the sky got my attention. The sun was gone, tucked behind a swatch of dark gray. The wind had picked up and it was fitting that some kind of apocalyptic storm would come and wash us all away.

With a heavy breath, I pushed myself to my feet. Swallowing the regret in my throat, I found some sort of resolve and moved forward like a zombie. I opened the gate and cringing, I pushed the cart through it.

Mike's head was leaning back. His empty eyes, staring up at a bleak sky that they would never see again. His hair moved slightly in the wind, giving the impression that there could still be life inside of him, but his bloodstained shirt told a different story.

As I neared my house I slowed down. I was thankful for the empty streets and shut windows that kept prying eyes from seeing me. I didn't know what to say, I didn't know how to explain what had happened and in a few short minutes I'd be face to face with a grieving wife and heartbroken children.

I stopped the cart one house away, out front of Jake's place and took several deep breaths. Jennifer didn't need to see this alone and I immediately thought of her dad, Mr. Spintz.

I wheeled Mike closer to my porch where he was obscured by the landscaping, then headed next door to Mike's house. If I was lucky, Jennifer would be busy with the kids and Mr. Spintz would answer the door, but my day had been anything but lucky.

I pressed the doorbell then stepped back. After a few moments, I heard rumbling inside and then the door swung open. Standing in front of me was Zach, Mike's seven-year-old son. He was the spitting image of his father and looking into his eyes sent a jolt to my heart that was almost debilitating.

"Hey Mr. Williams. Is my dad back yet?"

I choked up and tried to blink away the tears that burned with shame. "No," I grumbled in a rough voice. "No not yet. Can you get your grandpa?"

Zach nodded with a smile, then skipped away without a care in the world. This was going to be much harder than I imagined.

"Randall, where's Mike?" Jennifer's voice called as she headed toward the door.

"Um...I, I just need to see Mr. Spintz real quick."

"Is everything okay?"

"Yeah, everything is..."

"Randall," Mr. Spintz announced his presence.

He stopped behind Jennifer with a welcoming smile that was about to be ripped away. I looked up at him and stared into his eyes. His jaw tightened and his face changed.

Mr. Spintz was a military man, a Vietnam veteran and perhaps experiences like that gave you the ability to see the shadow of death on someone's face. Whatever it was he seemed to understand the severity without a word being spoken.

"Jennifer, can you grab Zach a cupcake? I need to have a word with Randall."

Jennifer looked a bit confused, but didn't question it. "Sure, but don't go too far boys."

Mr. Spintz smiled then stepped onto the porch and closed the door behind him. I took a few steps back and dropped my head. I couldn't stand to look at him, I couldn't stand to tell him that his son-in-law lay dead only a few feet away.

"What happened?" Mr. Spintz asked in a serious tone.

"Mr. Spintz...I, I..."

"George," he interrupted. "Call me George."

"George, I don't know where to begin."

"Is he dead?" George asked as if he needed confirmation.

My eyes answered him before my words ever could. His face pained and wrinkled, aged before my eyes. He too, thought of what the news would do to the family and I could see it tearing him apart.

"Did you, did you bring him back?" he asked.

I nodded then moved toward the steps. I motioned at the bushes and he followed after me. As Mike's body came into view he paused and stared at him from a distance.

Shaking his head from side to side, he collected himself. He walked next to the cart and placed his hand on Mike's leg.

"What happened?"

"It's bad out there George. A lot of looting at the store," I started.

I knew it would be hard for anyone to understand that hadn't seen it. Before we'd left, we thought it was just a power outage that would be over in a few days. The reality was the world, or at least our city was falling apart.

"It's not like we thought it was. The shopping center was on fire, people were everywhere. We grabbed as much stuff as we could and tried to leave, but some guys stopped us. One of them shot him," I finished and my voice broke.

"I feared it would get like this. It always gets like this," George replied.

What an odd thing to say, I thought. It seemed like George was even more paranoid than I was. But with Mike dead in the cart in front of him, I guess he had every reason to be.

"I tried George, he just wouldn't stop bleeding. He died right before the gate."

"This is gonna break her. The boys, the boys might not understand and good if they don't, but this is gonna break Jennifer. She'll never come back from this."

I didn't know how to reply. My heart ached for their family and the guilt that amplified inside of me was more than I could bear.

"Dad," Jennifer suddenly called from the porch. "He's right there boys."

Suddenly, Zach and their younger son, Max, hurried down the steps of the porch and ran toward us. Jennifer was a little ways behind them and had already started to twist her face, trying to figure out what George and I were looking at.

"No!" George shouted as he tried to head the boys off. "Jennifer keep them back."

Jennifer's face shown that she'd already recognized the lifeless mass that jutted out of the cart. Before words could leave her lips, she tore off toward us with her mouth gaping wide and her eyes beaming disbelief.

"Michael!" she screamed in a guttural, harrowing voice.

George tried to step in front of her, but she blew past him and charged toward the cart. I didn't know what to do so I just stood there in shock.

"Michael...what's wrong with him?" she wailed.

She fell forward on top of him and started crying uncontrollably. Her fingers found his face and she tried to lift his head. "Get up, get up Mike. Come on, we need to go inside. Somebody...call somebody. He needs me, he needs help."

As her emotions unraveled, she spiraled into a darkness that chilled my spine. Random words mixed with sobs and screeches of pain erupted like a popped balloon. The human mind couldn't comprehend death. It was an irrational aberration and the only response the brain knew was fear, anger and malfunction.

George grabbed her and she flung and kicked her legs wildly. Zach and Max stood by with stone faces, their immature brains trying to make sense of the lie their eyes told. I vaguely remember trying to usher them inside, but suddenly Jennifer escaped George's grasp and her pain turned to venom aimed in my direction.

"Don't you fucking touch them!" she shouted so loudly that people from several houses down had started to peek outside. "What did you do...what did you do to him? I hate you, I fucking hate you!"

She slapped me in the face then dove at me. I did nothing to protect myself. Whatever she was feeling, whatever she needed to do, I deserved. I'd taken her husband and there was nothing anyone could do to bring him back.

The door to my house slowly opened and Melinda stepped out. She silently surveyed the scene, trying to comprehend the madness that was ensuing before her. Her eyes locked onto Jennifer and she rushed down the steps, but froze when she spotted Mike's body.

By that time, Zach and Max were at their father's side, pulling on his arm. They looked scared and confused, but what really stung my heart was that they expected him to get up at any moment.

"Dad," Max's soft voice called. "Dad wake up."

With a pained face, Melinda walked toward them. "Come on guys, your dad isn't feeling well." As she led the boys away from the cart she glanced back at Mike's corpse and shuddered.

"Jennifer it's not his fault. You have to calm down," George groaned and grabbed her again.

As he pulled her away she swiped her hand and slashed me across the cheek with her nails. I felt the sensation of her fingers touching my face, but there was no pain. I was numb and having to watch a man's children plead over his dead body was more than I could take.

"I hate you! I hate you!" Jennifer screeched as George led her back inside.

Melinda took the boys into our house and for a short time I was alone. I stood on the sidewalk, staring up at the sky, questioning everything that I'd thought I knew just a few hours before.

More dark clouds had gathered in dense clusters, ready to burst. Gusts of cool wind blew across my face, but I found no pleasure in it. The sky grumbled at me angrily, protesting against the wrongs I had done

"Randall," George's voice called.

I slowly turned to face him, trying to hide the water on my face that had nothing to do with the incoming storm. Our eyes met and he understood the pain I felt and nodded his head in acceptance.

"It sounds wrong...but, they have a deep freezer in the garage. It's still pretty cold and it's empty. We need to move him. We can't leave him out here. Tomorrow, I'll notify the proper authorities."

I didn't reply. He was right, it did sound wrong. What had our world come to that a dead man had no better resting place than a meat freezer in his own garage?

61

A few days ago, he'd cleared that freezer out to make room for the deer he'd bring home from his annual hunting trip up north. A few days ago, he was busy planning a menu for the upcoming Super bowl party. A few days ago, he would've slept next to his wife, in his own bed with his children crammed in between them, not in a cold metal box.

"Randall," George called again. "We have to do this."

CHAPTER 8

THE DAY AFTER

I'd fallen asleep on the couch, staring out of the window. The next day when I awoke Melinda was gently snoring beside me, balled up under a blanket.

I gave her a soft nudge and she slowly opened her eyes. I immediately felt the stab in my heart that I thought I'd left with yesterday. I groaned and leaned forward with my elbows on my knees.

"You okay?" Melinda asked.

"No."

"What...what happened out there?"

I knew that question was coming and I was happy to have avoided it yesterday. But now I had no choice, but to deal with it. It would probably be the topic of discussion for the next few weeks and I was certain the police would be eager to hear what happened.

With a deep breath, I dove into the chilling tale at the grocery store. Melinda gasped and covered her mouth as I divulged the details and I did my best to paint Mike in a good light. He'd been overly aggressive that day, but nobody deserved to die for standing up to bullies.

When I finished, Melinda wiped the tears from her face and hugged me. It felt good to let my guard down, even for just a moment as I relaxed into her embrace. Yesterday's events had taken a toll on me, but they paled in comparison to what was ahead.

"I'm gonna wash up then go next door and see if George needs my help," I told her as I stood up and stretched.

"Okay, just be careful."

I nodded then headed into our room. Stepping into the shower I grabbed the bucket of water from the floor and poured it over my head. The cold water was like being doused with reality. My eyes snapped wide open and the gravity of what was going on came full front.

Mike had died and my biggest fear had been realized. I was helpless. There was no one to call, no doctor or paramedics to come save him. No police to come and protect us. I was living in modern day America and I had to push my neighbors dead body home in a grocery shopping cart.

I stood in the shower for a while, thinking about what all of those things meant. Wondering if this was a temporary jaunt in the twilight zone or had something changed within our society forever.

Without vehicles, without phones, we'd been cut off from the rest of the world. It was like we'd been marooned on an island and left to fend for ourselves. I wanted to know what was going on. I needed to know what was going on.

After half an hour, I got out and threw on some gym clothes. I headed out to the kitchen, where David and Charlie were up eating breakfast and Melinda was wiping the counters down, probably trying to keep her mind busy.

"Alistair get up yet?" I asked.

"He's still in his room...and that cart is still on the porch."

I nodded, knowing exactly why she'd told me that. It was something I had to deal with, but first I wanted to check on Alistair.

I gave David and Charlie a kiss on the head. They smiled and went back to their intense chat about what video game they'd play first, once the power was restored. At least they hadn't been affected by all of the madness, they still had hope.

After that I headed to Alistair's room and tapped on the door. He made some sound of acknowledgement and I walked in. He was lying on his back staring up at the ceiling, pondering the meaning of life most likely.

"What you up to?" I asked.

"Just chilling...Zach's dad died?"

I frowned and took a seat on the end of his bed. Like I thought, death would be the topic of conversation today.

"Yeah, how'd you know?" I replied.

"Saw the cart and all, out of the window. I've never seen a dead body."

"Me neither."

"What happened?"

"Some bad people at the grocery store."

"Scared people," he corrected me.

"What?"

"Scared people. They probably weren't bad before all of this, they're just scared and that makes them dangerous."

I looked at him and smiled. "Wise beyond your years. You gonna be okay?"

"Yeah, just sucks for Zach and Max."

"It does, but they're young. Kids are really resilient at that age."

Alistair grunted and shook his head. "Why do people always say that?"

"Say what?"

"They're young...like that's a good thing. Doesn't that make it worse? The older you get you expect your parents to die and you have a lifetime of memories with them. If you lose them as a kid...you might forget them."

"You'll never forget your parents. But sometimes not being able to fully comprehend something is a blessing in disguise. Like you right now, you're aware, you know what happened and it bothers

66

you. Your brothers don't have a clue and in that, they're happy because to them nothing bad ever existed."

"Dad, we can't live in the fairy tale forever."

"No, but you should try."

With that, I gave him a hug and told him I loved him. Alistair and I had a special bond and I was happy that I was able to talk to him in ways that I never could with my own father. I guess we strive to fix the issues from our childhood once we become parents. The idea of that gave me hope.

As I closed his door the grim reality of life returned. I still had to deal with today and everything that came with it.

I walked outside and stopped on the porch. Melinda must've dragged the cart up the few steps and tried to keep it out of sight. I knew that had to be hard because the metal frame gleamed with Mike's dried blood.

"Fuck," I grumbled.

It was like I was reliving that moment all over again. The vivid images of Mike pleading for help rushed to the front of my mind. I shivered as goose bumps erupted across my arms and wondered how long it would haunt me.

Cringing, I started sifting through the contents of the buggy. The lunch meat was bad so I threw that out first. Then I tried grabbing items that hadn't been showered in blood.

The more things I moved around the more blood poured from the bottom of the cart and splattered onto the porch. Without running water, I was forced to use some of the water jugs to clean everything off. Although I had a generous amount of water stored in my house, that was one of the things you could never have too much of.

As I cleaned off the last of the cans and set it down near the front door, I heard what sounded like a semi-truck. A bit of hope rose in my chest as imagined it was the power companies or first responders finally making their way out.

I started towards the steps, but as I made my way down I dropped to the floor and covered my head. An explosion suddenly shook the air and my eardrums popped. I could feel the wave of air rush past me.

Recovering, I jumped up and ran to the sidewalk. I peered down the road toward the gate and stopped in shock. "Holy shit!"

CHAPTER 9

THE WELCOMING PARTY

I stepped to the side as the heavy armored vehicle slowly wheeled past me. Behind it, rows and rows of troops trotted at a moderate pace. They were all dressed in sand colored fatigues with rifles at the ready.

"What the hell was that noi..," Melinda's words fell short as her eyes found the small army outside.

I looked back at her with wild eyes. I couldn't believe what I was seeing and I felt frozen with shock and fear. We needed help, but not this, this was an occupying force. I felt like a small child watching the Army roll into Baghdad.

"Over there," I heard someone behind me call out.

I turned and there was a middle-aged man heading my way. Like the other soldiers, he was dressed in fatigues, but his rifle was slung over his back. He had another five troops with him, following like hand maids or something.

"Sir," he shouted before he was close enough to talk in a normal voice.

"Yeah," I replied casually. Then I considered how strange I must have looked with a blood-stained t-shirt and a shopping cart on the porch behind me.

"My name is Captain Swonski," he said and extended his hand.

I reached out and shook it then he looked me over. He tried to hide the surprise in his face, but I already knew what was coming next.

"What happened here?" he asked.

"My neighbor was murdered yesterday," I admitted reluctantly.

I prepared myself for the lengthy interrogation that I knew was coming. I prepared to take him next door, into the garage to the body. I didn't know how I could talk myself out of what would happen next, but I was ready to take the blame.

But he didn't press me any further. No questions or even second looks. He shook his head like he completely understood and that made my spine chill.

"How many residents are in this community?" he continued.

"I don't know. Are you guys with the national guard or something? Did they declare some kind of disaster?"

"Not quite," he replied. "I need to speak with your community leader. We need to round everyone together...is there some sort of town hall or meeting room?"

"What? What the hell are you talking about?"

I didn't mean to come off so rudely, but the entire thing took me a bit by surprise. There was a freaking military force parked on my street and it suddenly dwarfed every other problem I had.

"What's your name?" he asked with a hint of suspicion in his voice.

"Randall," I replied.

"Well look Randall," he began.

"Sir," another soldier called. He approached the captain and saluted then extended a clipboard with a stack of papers. "One hundred and sixty-two sir. We double checked. No meeting hall."

"Very well, " the captain told him. "We'll have to go door to door. Lieutenant, move them out."

"Yes sir," the Lieutenant said as he saluted then turned on his heels.

Swonski let out a long breath then turned back to me. "Randall, I'll have to ask that you stay inside. Someone will be by shortly with more details."

"What? Stay inside...what the hell is going on?"

"Someone will explain shortly. I have to ask, for your safety though, that you and your family remain in your residence. Is that understood?"

I wanted to protest, but the captain had the type of face that you didn't argue with. He had dark eyes and thick, brown eyebrows that created a shadow effect. I suspected that even his smile looked like an ill-wishing scowl and I didn't want to be on his bad side this early.

"I'll wait here," I replied. "But I want to know what's going on."

Swonski nodded then headed back out into the street. I watched him for a moment, feeling a nervous apprehension. I'd been waiting for power companies and emergency workers, but instead an occupying force showed up. Something really bad was going on and I was starting to doubt that things were gonna go back to how they were.

"What was that about?" Melinda asked as I ushered her back inside.

Once the door was closed and locked I pulled her into the living room. We both had a seat on the couch and I leaned back and let out a long, rattled sigh.

"We have to get out of here," I said after I collected my thoughts.

"What was that out there?"

"I don't know. The military, the national guard maybe, I'm not sure. Something wasn't right with that guy though. And he was asking how many residents were here."

"Makes sense if they are trying to account for people. Randall, you think everything is some kind of conspiracy."

"Melinda, they didn't come with food and water. They came with fucking tanks and guns."

"Keep your voice down!" she warned. "I don't want the kids hearing you."

"Something is going on and I don't think it's safe to stay here. This feels wrong, feels like we're in some third world country all of a sudden."

"Even if we could leave Randall, where would we go? The cars don't work and you don't have any clue what's going on out there. The last time you left..." she stopped herself and covered her mouth. "I'm sorry."

I frowned and lowered my head. "I don't know Melinda, but I'm worried. We need to get out of here and find out what's really going on. We could make it to the news station or take one of those boats in the harbor and just get the hell out of here."

Melinda started to respond, but a knock at the door cut her off. We looked at each other and her eyes reflected mine, surprise and fear. I gave her a weak smile, then got up and walked to the door.

The knock sounded again. This time more urgently and I wanted to grab my family and run off rather than open it.

"I'm coming," I said.

Swallowing, I unlocked the door and cracked it. Greg was standing on the porch looking nervous and scared. Without a word, he rushed inside.

I closed the door behind him then turned around. "Everything okay?"

"Did you see...did you see what's going on out there?" he asked with a trembling voice.

"You mean with the army or whatever?"

"They're taking people!"

"What!?" I snapped and looked back at Melinda.

"You heard what happened to Mike right? I can't believe it man." He lowered his head and seemed lost in his thoughts for a moment.

"I was there."

"Holy shit! I'm sorry man," he sighed and rubbed his hands across his face. "Fucking Mike...can't, can't believe he's gone. Wait! You told them that...they know you were with him? They're gonna come here. They're gonna take you too."

"Greg chill out. What are you talking about?"

At this point, Greg was looking around the house with crazy eyes and waving his hands hysterically. He looked like a mad man and I could tell he was on the verge of completely losing his shit.

"They went to Mike's house...took them all."

"Well, Mike's dead. They had to do something and they probably took his family to help them."

"George was fighting them. Jennifer and the kids were screaming like hell. That doesn't sound like help to me."

I twisted my face in surprise. "Swonski didn't seem all that interested in what had happened to Mike when I told him about it."

"Who?"

Suddenly, there was another knock at the door. Greg froze then started searching the house for a place to hide.

"It's them!" he said frantically. "They can't find me here. I have to go!"

Greg sprinted through the house to the sliding glass door. He yanked it open and rushed through the lanai into the backyard. Tripping over toys, he darted through the hedges and vanished.

I stared after him for a few minutes to make sure he was gone then headed to the door. He was right. I opened the door and Captain Swonski and a few of his men were gathered on my porch.

"Do you mind if we come in?" he asked.

I looked them over as if I had any choice in the matter. Grunting, I nodded and stepped to the side. The captain and his men stepped inside and I led them to the living room where Melinda was still sitting.

"This is your wife?" he asked.

"Yes. So, what's going on?"

He didn't answer immediately. He walked toward the back window and stared out into the yard. He seemed to be searching and I could tell, he was the type of man that was used to finding what he looked for.

"Captain," I said with a slightly raised voice. "What is all of this about?"

He turned and came back to where we were sitting. He took a deep breath then sat down in a chair across from us.

"Do you people have any clue of what is going on?"

I laughed even though I didn't mean to. "No... that's what I'm asking you," I replied. "People are looting the stores, killing people. We have no phones, no electricity, no water. And then the army shows up. No, I don't have any clue what's going on."

The captain looked tired. I could see the strain in his eyes along with broken red lines that webbed across his pupils. He looked weighed down with thoughts, thoughts of things I wasn't aware of.

"Civil unrest is just the tip," he said in a labored voice. "These...these weather anomalies are only going to get worse."

"Weather anomalies?" I asked.

"We...we were supposed to be ahead of it all. Evacuations and the plans we made should have worked, should've kept them safe."

He was talking to himself, staring straight ahead with unfocused eyes. It was like he'd forgotten he was in my house.

"They weren't safe and now we have to do this. Things will only get worse if we don't do this."

"Do what?" I asked.

His face hardened and his eyes focused as he stood up. He shook his head from side to side as if to rid himself of the bout of empathy he'd just had.

"We are here to maintain order, to keep the peace and ensure that nothing happens...that nothing else happens. Soldiers will be stationed at the gates as well as at posts along the streets. Stay in your homes as much as possible and we'll sort this out."

"What about the weather?" I asked again.

"That will be all Randall," he said and then walked out of the door with his guards.

CHAPTER 10

OCCUPYING BY FORCE

"What do you think they want?" Melinda asked as we sat at the dining room table.

"I don't know. To keep everyone in check...it's martial law I guess. I mean after what I saw at the store, it's not that hard to believe."

I pushed around the sliced hot dog in front of me and rolled it through the ketchup. This was the fifth day in a row that a grilled hot dog and corn on the cob was dinner. I guess it could be worse, but my stomach missed the disastrous taste of fast food.

"You hear that?" Melinda asked and broke me out of my McDonalds nostalgia.

"What?"

As soon as I asked I heard a faint scream outside. I waited, straining my ears and then I heard it again.

"Sounds like it's across the street," I said and stood up.

I glanced at Melinda and then started toward the door. As I got closer two more screams rang out and then a man shouted something I couldn't make out.

"Dad, what is that?" Alistair asked and poked his head out of his room.

"I'm not sure. I'll be right back."

I stepped outside and immediately saw the source of all the noise. Across the street our neighbors, Sue and Debbie, the two nurses, were wrestling with one of the soldiers. Two more soldiers were standing on the sidewalk, watching them with mild interest.

"Calm down!" the soldier said and held Debbie's wrist while he kept Sue at bay with his outstretched hand.

"We're not going anywhere!" Debbie screamed. "You can't just make people leave their house."

"Ma'am it's not safe."

"For the love of God Jackson, just throw the bitches in the truck and let's get moving already," one of the soldiers on the sidewalk said. He was a short guy with a foul look on his face and slicked back red hair.

Jackson waved him off. "Ma'am please, I'm trying to help you. We're trying to get you somewhere safe."

"Get off of her," Sue yelled and jumped on Jackson's back.

The other soldier had seen all he could take. " Hey!" he shouted.

Jumping forward, he grabbed Sue by her collar and yanked her to the ground. She landed flat on her back and let out a rattled grunt. Her head smashed into the concrete and she reeled across the floor in pain.

"Calm down!" he shouted and brought his open hand crashing down on Debbie's face.

She screeched then dropped to her knees in tears.

"Jesus, Tolbert what the hell was that for?" Jackson asked as he straightened up.

"These crazy chicks need to get a grip. I told you we don't' have time for this."

He grabbed Debbie by the hair and pulled her up. Sue was still trying to regain her senses and he didn't seem to pay her much attention.

"You're gonna get your shit and come with us. Do you understand that?"

"Hey!" I yelled as my feet took me forward. "What the fuck are you assholes doing? You can't treat people like this."

I had spouted a mouthful before I even knew what I was saying. My legs shook with anger as I walked toward them and I wasn't even sure why I was so mad.

"Excuse me," Tolbert said.

I could see the unnamed soldier place his hand on the rifle that hung around his neck. This reminded me why I always minded my own damn business.

"You can't beat people...this ain't Iraq!" I shouted hoping my loud voice would at least gain the interest of a few witnesses.

"You better go back inside before I show you just how we treat people in Iraq."

"That's enough Tolbert, we'll come back later," Jackson said and stepped in between us.

"No! These ladies are gonna pack up and we're gonna finish our job. And this dickless asshole," he nodded at me. "He's gonna go back inside before I shove a boot up his ass."

"What size do you wear?" the question left my mouth before I could swallow it back.

The soldier gripping his rifle cracked a smile and Jackson laughed. That only made Tolbert all the more angry.

He let go of Debbie and steamed toward me. Biting his lower lip, he grabbed me by the shirt collar and pulled me forward. I could smell the stench of onions and cigarettes on his breath.

"Look you little fuck," he growled.

"Sergeant!" Swonski shouted from behind me.

Tolbert dropped me and snapped to attention. As I caught my breath, I turned around and found the captain gazing at me with a beet red face.

"What the hell is going on here?"

"Sir, nothing sir."

Debbie clambered to her feet and then dove at Tolbert. "You piece of shit!" she screamed.

Jackson wrapped his arms around her shoulders and held her back. Sue was still trying to gather herself and I was trying to make sense of the whole situation.

"Randall, please forgive my men. They tend to get a bit overzealous," Swonski said. "This...this business makes us all a bit restless."

"And what business is that?" I asked accusingly.

Swonski squinted his eyebrows and shot me daggers. "You can return home now. This won't happen again."

He stepped toward me and brought himself to his full height. I wanted to punch him, but I knew that would end bad for me. Grinding my teeth, I cast one more dirty look at Tolbert then headed back to my house.

CHAPTER 11

DE OPPRESSO LIBER

Days passed with Captain Swonski and his men monitoring us like we were in prison. No one was allowed to leave the neighborhood and we hadn't heard anything else about what was happening outside. It was disturbing how quickly people learned to tolerate, even accept oppression. It's little battles that are lost daily and you never even notice how far you've fallen, until you've lost everything.

More families had been taken without a word, including Jake and Trent. It seemed completely random, but I knew there had to be more going on. Every morning I wondered who would be the next person to vanish.

Greg and I had begun to have secret meetings late at night to discuss what news if any we'd learned that day. Normally it was nothing, but sometimes we'd manage to piece together enough, to paint a pretty grim picture of what the world had become.

"Eddie heard one of the troops talking...says he thinks they'll be leaving soon," Greg said as we sat at my dining room table under dim light.

"What does that mean?"

"Can't mean anything good. He just said he heard them say they'd be moving out."

"And what about the people that were at the gate?"

"Gone, they didn't let them in and I don't think they were too nice about getting rid of them, at least that's what I heard."

Rumors and "he said she said" is what we'd been reduced to. But at least it was something. The military wasn't all bad though. They'd provided food and water and even had a few gas burners that allowed us to cook actual food. But things weren't getting any better and I was still pushing the agenda to leave.

We wrapped up our secret meeting and Greg snuck back home. After that I checked on the kids then locked up and went to bed.

The next morning I awoke to the sound of drums beating at the door. Melinda was already wide awake, staring around with crazed eyes and rambling on about something I couldn't immediately understand.

"Go check the door!" she said again and her words finally made sense.

I crawled out of the bed and stumbled toward the door. The knocking hadn't let up and I was starting to feel a chill creep down my spine. It was a frantic sound, like someone was trying to get in.

"I'm coming!" I yelled.

A little annoyed, I yanked the door open. Greg was standing there with a crazy look in his eyes.

"They left!" he said.

"What?"

"The military, they left. Every last one of them."

I scratched my head and stepped onto the porch. I didn't see any soldiers so I ventured further out and walked down the steps. I stopped in the street and looked from side to side.

"When did they leave?"

"I don't know, but they're gone. They packed up everything. I checked outside of the gate, there's not a sign of them anywhere."

Greg was right, there wasn't a troop in sight and all of their equipment and vehicles were gone. I should've been happy they'd left us, but it made me wonder just what could've occurred that caused them to pack up and leave town.

"I don't think it's a good thing," I said to Greg.

"Who knows? I didn't like them around here, that's for sure. A bunch of guys with guns is never a good thing."

For the next few days things did seem to get better. People were outside more often, there was less talk of doom and gloom, and the best part was the military had left all of the supplies they'd brought.

But after a while the portable toilets became full, the gas grills ran out of propane and the pallets of water ran dry. Suddenly, we were back to scavenging, to struggling to survive and the optimistic attitude evaporated like a puddle of water.

"It's been three weeks," Melinda said in desperation. "We have to do something."

"I said we should leave, but you don't want to. What else do you want me to do?" I asked.

"Why can't you just fix the car? They had those jeeps and they worked."

I sighed. "Whatever messed up our stuff didn't mess up everything. And I don't know how to fix a car anyway. We just need to get out of here Melinda. The longer we stay the harder its gonna be to find some place safe. We still don't have a clue what's really going on out there, but the military left and they must've had good reason."

"Dad's right," Alistair added. He'd just walked out of his room and was standing in the hall watching us. "I think we should leave...this is getting scary."

I'd never seen Alistair like that before. He was normally a serious kid, but optimistic and full of bright ideas. Now, he looked defeated and pained.

"I don't know," Melinda replied. "I just don't know."

She huffed then got up and headed into our bedroom. Alistair came and took a seat next to me and we just stared out of the open window into the backyard.

A cool breeze blew in and I considered grabbing a light jacket, but the weather was so scarcely chilly that I decided to soak it in. Brown, dead leaves fell from the lone tree out back and the wide, brick wall that separated the back of our neighborhood from the highway could be seen clearly.

I thought about what was going on in the world outside. Three weeks was a long time to be cut off from everything. It was a long time to not hear the news or the ring of a phone. It was a long time to be alone.

"Where would we go?" Alistair asked in a light voice.

"I don't know...away from here. I guess it depends on what it's really like out there."

"You think it's gotten worse?""

"Yeah, I think so."

"You think it'll ever be the same again?"

I looked at Alistair then lowered my gaze. I never lied to him, but at the same time I knew how horrible the answer would sound. The same fear he felt, I'd been hiding for a long time. Something had happened and I didn't think our world would ever be the same again. Beyond that, I feared leaving our house and neighborhood, but I'd rather know what's waiting around the corner. Staying there was just avoiding reality and dying slowly.

"Alistair, I don't know. I hope it will, but the more I see the more I feel like we may have reached a point where there's no going back."

Alistair frowned. He nodded his head slightly and took a deep breath. "Me too."

"Dad!" Charlie suddenly shouted.

I jumped up and sprinted toward their room. I almost tore my ACL whipping around the corner, but I came to a stop in their doorway with Melinda right behind me.

"What's wrong?" I huffed.

"My iPad...it's working," he said in excitement.

"What?" I reached out and grabbed the little silver tablet.

The light in the corner flashed and then something blinked across the screen and it went off. I glanced at Melinda with excitement in my eyes.

"Is it working?" Melinda asked.

"I think it was," I said as I depressed the power button over and over with no success.

"You broke it!" David shot.

"Shut up David. Charlie, what did you do to get it to work?"

"Nothing, it...it just started working."

Shaking my head, I handed the tablet back to him. "Let me know if it happens again."

"Randall!" Greg's voice shouted from the front door as he hammered it loudly.

"What now?" I grumbled.

I left Melinda with the kids and ran to get the door. As soon as I opened it Greg bolted inside, nearly knocking me over.

"What the hell is wrong with you?"

"People..." he huffed as he tried to catch his breath. "Guns, they...got... guns."

Confused, I bent the blind on the front window and glanced outside. Several men armed with hunting rifles and pistols were trotting down the middle of the road. They looked like they were trying to imitate a military patrol, but it was obvious they didn't have the training.

"Holy shit!" I mumbled and shuffled backward.

"What's going on?" Melinda asked from behind me.

I put my finger to my mouth then locked the door. Melinda gave me a confused look and tilted her head. I grabbed her by the arm and moved further into the house as I looked at her with an intensity that I hope she comprehended.

"There are people with guns outside. Not soldiers, just people," I whispered.

"Yeah, some kind of militia," Greg added as he found his voice.

"We need to go...we need to go now!" I said.

Melinda shook her head from side to side and started to say something. The crackle of a gunshot sent her diving to the floor with a high-pitched yelp.

I took off running toward the kid's room. They were sitting on the bed trying to get their iPad to work again. As I stormed through the door I dove and tackled them both to the ground.

Charlie let out an odd sounding chirp and David laughed and started punching at me like we were playing a game.

"Guys, be very quiet okay."

"Hide and go seek?" David asked with an excited grin.

"No this is serious. Bad people are outside. Be very quiet and follow me."

Their faces changed, mirroring my concern. I dropped to all fours and they did the same. We crawled across the floor as quickly as we could until we were back in the living room with Melinda and Greg.

"Did you hear that?" Alistair asked as he came sliding around the corner.

"Get down!" I shouted.

Another gunshot shattered the air then screams followed. They were close, no more than a few houses away. I didn't know what was going on, but I knew we needed to get out of the neighborhood and fast.

"Melinda, we are leaving! Grab their bags and load up as much from the pantry as you can. Alistair help her," I said in an urgent voice.

Greg was still cowering on the floor, looking terrified. Reluctantly, he pushed himself to all fours and looked over at me.

"Where are you going?" he asked.

"Away from here."

"I'm coming," he replied.

I nodded then rushed to the closet to grab my bug out bag and anything else I could cram into it. My hands trembled with panic as I tried to yank down the zipper, then I reached inside and pulled out the small, metal gun safe at the bottom. Moving quickly, I opened it and grabbed the black, pistol inside.

I stared at it, wishing I'd gone to the gun range or at least watched a YouTube video on how to use it. I'd always assumed the internet would be around, who knows how the world got along before it. But that was a question for another day, I grunted and crammed the gun into my waistline.

"Hurry up!" Greg called.

Rushing, I stuffed more water and meal rations into the orange and gray nylon. Then I tied up the tent I'd purchased at Wal-Mart and slung the entire thing onto my back.

I stood there for a moment. It was funny that the few supplies I'd bought after watching some doomsday movie were now going to decide if I lived or died. The idea of a world where the simple things like running water or electricity didn't exist, previously stood at the far reaches of my unconscious mind. Now, this was my reality and accepting that became the most sobering moment that I could remember.

I'd told myself a lie my whole life, we all had. We'd built our cities and highways, giant, cascading statues of steel. We'd connected the far reaches of the world with technology, able to send messages across the globe in the blink of an eye. We'd created a central nervous system for all humans, a knowledge repository so vast that it could only exist in space.

And through all of that we'd forgotten how to live. That was my fear. That I would take my family into the unknown and let them die. That after years of fast food and comfy chairs and computers, I wouldn't be able to provide the basics. That we'd die of thirst or starve to death because of my ineptitude, because of my inability to be a man.

Loud shouts and screams from outside brought me back to the moment. I shut the closet door and hurried back to the living room. Melinda was already there, trying to comfort David and Charlie. They were terrified and while they couldn't completely understand the danger, they were perceptive enough to know that they should be afraid.

"It's gonna be okay," Melinda said over and over.

"We are going on a mission," I started. "I need you guys to stay close and be very quiet. When we run, you run. When we stop, you stop. You guys understand?"

They both nodded. I looked at Alistair and he stared back at me with an intense resolve on his face. I was impressed, he didn't break easily.

"Ready?" Melinda asked.

Suddenly, there was a knock on the door and everyone froze. Melinda looked at me with a fear in her eyes that coiled around my neck and squeezed. She wrapped her arms around the kids and lowered to the floor.

"If you're in there, come out now or we are coming in!" a deep barreled voice shouted.

The door shook as they beat on it again and then the knob began to rattle loudly. My hand drifted to the pistol stuck in my pants and I swallowed the fear at the back of my throat.

"Go through the back," Greg suddenly said.

"What?"

"Take them through the back and over the wall. The drop is only five feet or so on that side. I'll get rid of the guys on the porch."

I looked out of the back window and stared at the tan, brick wall that spanned the length of the neighborhood. Because of the incline at the back of the house it was only two feet to stand on top of the wall, but it dropped off to ground level on the other side.

"Are you sure? What are you gonna do?" I asked.

"Yeah, I'll ditch them. Give them what they want then I'll meet you on the other side."

The door rattled again then started to buckle as the men outside began to kick it. I grabbed Melinda by the hand and smiled.

"Go now!" Greg grunted through gritted teeth.

"Be safe," I told him and patted him on the shoulder.

Then I turned back to Melinda and the kids. I could see the fear and trepidation written in tears on their faces. I could also see the trust they'd put in me to get them through whatever was going to happen.

They had their bags strapped tightly on their backs. Their running shoes laced up and their jackets pulled snug.

I looked back around the house and deep inside I knew it would be the last time I was there. A lifetime of memories lingered in the halls and I felt like I was leaving a piece of me behind.

I took a deep breath and summoned all of the resolve I could find. I was at the edge of a great decision, a journey that would test our will to live. I could only hope that we were ready. With more fear than bravery, I turned toward the back door. I reached out for the handle and nodded at Greg. Staring back at my family, I managed a half smirk then willed myself forward and growled, "Let's go."

CHAPTER 12

THE GET AWAY

I ushered David and Charlie up the slight hill and we stopped next to Alistair and Melinda. I leaned over and stared down the side of the wall. Greg hadn't been that off, but the seven foot drop to the ground could mean a sprained ankle, which was something I didn't need.

"I'm gonna lower you down first Alistair and then you can help everyone else," I told him as I laid my bag in the grass.

Alistair smirked and before I could do anything else he scaled the wall and landed softly on the other side. I cut my eyes at him then grabbed Charlie and started to lower him down. After that went David and then I prepared to help Melinda over the wall.

Suddenly, there was a loud shout from the front and then a series of gunshots. Melinda screeched and tried to catch herself, but her grip loosened and she slipped from my hands.

"Melinda!" I yelled.

She tumbled backward as I lunged forward, grasping empty air. Alistair quickly moved toward the wall with outstretched arms. He caught her and they both flopped into the grass and rolled over.

"We're okay," he shouted.

I took a sigh of relief, then turned my head toward the crackling gunfire. There were more shouts and screams then a staccato of exploding bullets. Then there was silence.

I waited for what felt like hours. Hoping, wishing that Greg was okay. I could still feel the sting of Mike's death and I couldn't take another. The feeling of responsibility weighed me down like sandbags, like I was sending men to die for my own agenda.

"Come on...come on," I mumbled hopelessly.

With a remorseful sigh, I grabbed the bags and tossed them over the wall. Then I looked back one last time out of desperation. Guilt swelled in my throat and I choked, before swallowing it down like bitter poison.

I stared down at Melinda and frowned, shaking my head from side to side. I threw a leg over the wall then paused.

"Randall!" someone called.

I whipped my head around and Greg was running down the side of the house with a greedy, smile on his face. I felt my shoulders loosen and my chest expand freely. I'd never been so relieved in my life.

"What the hell happened up there?" I asked as he made it to the wall.

He had a bag on his back and his hand was pressing on a bloody wound on his shoulder. He laughed and climbed up on the top of the wall next to me.

"I'll tell you later, we need to go," he replied then slipped off of the wall and landed on the other side.

Feeling a bit of my anxiety creep back in, I followed after him. I landed awkwardly, but managed to recover without breaking anything. I shot an exhausted glance at Alistair then straightened up and grabbed my bag.

Melinda and the kids had already strapped up and were ready to go. They were staring around anxiously, watching the road like some evil force was about to manifest in the middle of it.

"Let's head across the street, we need to get the hell away from here," I said then turned to Greg. "Are you okay man?"

"Yeah, yeah I'm good. One of those bastards shot me in the shoulder. But no biggie...it barely hurts."

I looked at him skeptically, but I didn't have time to argue with him. I could hear the group of bandits starting to move around toward another house. I nodded my head at the highway and we got moving.

We quickly crossed the desolate street and ran past an abandoned church. There wasn't a sign of life anywhere.

Everything looked eerie, magnified by the long, stretch of empty road, but I didn't have time to ponder on that. We were running for our lives.

We moved into the forest that I'd driven past hundreds of times. It was a collection of Oak trees and tropical plants that grew thick in some sections, but for the most part it was manageable. If we avoided the rattlesnakes and coyotes we'd be alright.

The cool weather was nice. Normally the mosquitoes would be swarming all over the muggy, damp area, but falling temperatures had driven them away.

It was a little after midday and I figured we could get deep enough into the woods to make camp without being seen. Our best bet was to stay hidden. I'd been camping a few times before and felt confident in my ability to survive off the grid for a day or two.

Charlie and David were starting to come around. This was turning into more of an adventure for them than the reality of struggling to survive. They talked and sang little songs as we walked, which lightened the mood a bit and gave me an optimistic feeling.

Alistair didn't share in their childish utopia. He scanned the path in front of us like a hawk, snapping and turning his head with every sound. He knew enough to be scared and for once I wished he was still consumed with the kind of ignorance that only a kid could have.

Thin branches and dry grass crackled with every step we took as we pushed our way further and further into the undeveloped land.

Birds and insects whistled in high pitches like a nature soundtrack. Other than that, it was a silent journey, a time for me to think and clear my head.

Maybe this was the way things were supposed to be all along. Humans had spent too much time cooped up in houses and hidden behind desks. We were meant to be out in nature and even though I was afraid of how we'd get along, I felt like I belonged out here.

Once we'd walked for a mile or so there was enough trees between us and the road. Besides that, I was certain if we went much further I wouldn't be able to find my way back out.

Dropping my bag in a small clearing, I turned back to Melinda and said, "I think we'll stop here."

"Good...my legs hurt," she replied.

Greg groaned and dropped his gear as well then moved his arm around a bit, like he needed to make sure it still worked. The kids took a seat on top of their bags and Melinda gave them a bottled water and some chips. Alistair stared off into the thicket, like a hunting dog. If it were possible, he seemed more concerned about our bleak future than I did.

"What the hell happened back there? I heard shooting," I turned to Greg and asked.

Greg grinned, but even through that I could see the pain in his face. At a quick glance, the wound didn't look that bad, but he was sweating more than any of us and his skin looked like it had lost some color.

"I made it back to my house, packed up a few things," he started. "Told the guys they could have everything inside. Then they wanted my bag, we got into a bit of a tussle. One of em shot me, but I'm all good."

"Yeah, you need to take care of that. Let me clean it up and put a bandage or something over it."

I reached into my bag and pulled out the bottle of disinfectant I'd gathered from the store. I twisted off the cap and tipped it toward his arm. He jokingly slapped at my hand.

"Nah, that's gonna sting. Trust me I'm good, it's not even bleeding anymore."

"Look man, I'm no doctor or anything, but if you haven't noticed, it's not like we can just head to a hospital. If that gets infected or something...and did the bullet even come out?"

"I'm fine man, I really am."

I gave him a skeptical look, but let it go. He was a grown man after all and who was I to be giving any kind of survival advice. My knowledge came from shit I saw on the Discovery channel.

"We're gonna camp here and then head out in the morning," I said and started to unroll my tent.

"It's kinda early isn't it?" Greg asked.

"Yeah, but I don't want to be stumbling around the woods in the dark. We can start early tomorrow and get going."

"And where exactly are we going?"

"I've been thinking about that. With guys like we saw back in the neighborhood roaming around I don't think it's safe to be near the roads. I don't have a clue what's going on, but the safest place has to be MacDill."

"The air force base?" Alistair asked.

"Yep, those military guys from earlier knew something and if they packed up and left we should probably follow them."

"How are we gonna get there?" Melinda chimed in. "It's gotta be at least thirty miles and David and Charlie can't walk that far."

I smiled and held back for a moment. My genius plan was about to be revealed, but it felt kind of good being the mastermind behind everything.

Melinda gave me a look and huffed. I winked at her then cleared my throat.

"The harbor," I finally said.

"What harbor?" Greg asked as if my plan was the dumbest thing he'd ever heard.

"Any harbor, shit there's tons of them. We moved out here for the water and there's boats everywhere. The base is right across the bay. Wouldn't take us more than an hour or two to get there."

"You couldn't fix the car Randall, how the hell are you gonna get a boat to run?" Melinda jabbed.

"We take a sail boat. There's tons of them moored less than four miles from here."

"And who's gonna sail it?"

"What?" I asked and looked at her with squinting eyes.

"A sail boat Randall, they have sails and things. Who's gonna operate that? It's not as easy as it sounds and if you screw it up, we all drown."

I felt the air whistle from my chest and I slumped my shoulders. As simple as it was I hadn't thought of that and I sure as hell didn't know how to sail a boat, but how hard could it be?

"Look Melinda, if that's our only issue then I say we've made out. They're killing people back in our neighborhood. I'll take my chances in the water."

"I'm hungry!" David suddenly announced, which was immediately echoed by Charlie.

"I'll get the tent set up, you figure out dinner," I said and looked at Melinda.

"Well that's easy, we're going with lasagna or chicken and mash potatoes," she laughed and held up a package of freeze dried food.

Winking, I turned around and grabbed the tent. Alistair started unpacking the poles and Greg grabbed his own little pop-up tent and went to work. An hour later Greg was relaxing inside of his tent and me and Alistair were still trying to figure out which part was the floor.

"I thought you had instructions for that?" Melinda asked.

"Yeah, well we were kinda busy rushing out of the house from the damn murder brigade so I didn't grab them."

"Don't get mad at me, it's not my fault. And dinner is ready."

Melinda had used our little gas burner to heat up some water and make an edible version of chicken and mash potatoes. The kids must've been starving because they ate three helpings each and licked the flimsy plates when they were done.

After that me and Alistair went back to work on the tent. We managed to sort out the floor, but the poles were another story. Every time we set one up another fell over.

"Need some help?" Greg asked with a grin.

"Don't you start shit too," I replied.

He shrugged then winced. "Suit yourself."

Ignoring him, I went back to work. I was determined to get the tent up without outside intervention, besides I had a lot of faith in Alistair, he had a knack for things like this.

"What do you think?" I asked him.

"I think it took you too long to ask me for help."

"Well, now I am so you wanna take the lead on this or what?"

Alistair smiled. He grabbed a few poles and started arranging them around the flooring. Then he threaded them through some loops and grabbed the string. Twenty minutes later we had a fully functioning tent.

David and Charlie crawled inside just as the sun started to set. Within minutes they were snoring loudly while the rest of us sat around outside.

I used the flint rock in my bag and a knife to start a small fire. The temperature wasn't unbearable yet, but it was cool enough that a fire would make it comfortable.

"Do you think someone will see it?" Alistair questioned as he stared into the flames.

I looked up at the canopy of trees and billowing smoke. "If they were looking for it, but it's a full moon and I don't think those guys are worried about us any longer."

"What do you think is going on?" Melinda asked.

With a huff, I gazed into the flickering orange waves and thought about my answer. Everything was speculation at this point and the only thing that I knew was that I was missing the comfort of my own house.

"Terrorist attack," I replied.

Unoriginal, but certainly on the high list of probabilities. The captain had brought something up about weather, but that just didn't seem to fit. Storms were as much a part of Florida as sunshine. Anarchy and total power loss on the other hand, were new.

"You really think so?" Greg asked.

I nodded and poked at the fire with a stick. "What else could it be?"

"Hell...civil war, alien invasion, giant meteor, the list goes on."

"Climate change," Alistair added.

I gave him a sideways glance and shrugged. "How's the arm Greg?"

"I told you I'm fine. It's a little stiff, but I'm good."

"Well, I say we get to bed and get moving early morning. By this time tomorrow we could be in real beds."

"Wishful thinking, but I am tired," Greg replied.

I rolled my eyes then put out the fire and packed up. We said our goodnights then we all headed to bed.

Along with Melinda and Alistair, I crawled into our tent with David and Charlie. It was pretty large, with dividers that broke it into three rooms. The floor wouldn't be as comfortable as a bed, but we had some comfy sleeping bags that would be put to good use.

The cooling air was perfect. Crickets chirped a melodic lullaby and when combined with the stress from the day, it didn't take long before I was out cold.

The next day Melinda woke me up before the sun. Groaning, I slipped out of the tent and stretched. My back ached and I quickly realized a sleeping bag and uneven, rocky soil was no substitute for a place to sleep.

"I started breakfast," she said and pointed toward a pot steaming on the gas burner. "Oatmeal."

I smiled. "I could get use to this."

"I can't."

Sighing, I gave her a hug and rubbed her shoulders. "How are you doing?"

She looked back to make sure the kids were still sleeping. "I'm scared...real scared."

"Saying it'll be okay sounds too cliché. But we'll be alright, whatever is going on...we'll be alright. We'll stick together and get through this."

Melinda started to cry and I pulled her head into my chest. It broke my heart, I knew there was nothing I could say or do to comfort her. For the first time, everything she feared was legitimate and even worse, I was just as scared as she was.

"What are we gonna do Randall? Where is everyone? What is going on?"

"I don't know babe. We're gonna get to the base and figure it out from there."

She wrapped her arms around me and squeezed. I could feel her heart hammering in her chest and her hands quivering as she gripped my sides.

"I thought help would come. I thought they'd send someone," she sobbed.

With a grimace, I wiped the tears from her face and kissed her forehead. It pained me to see her that way. All I could do was keep telling myself that things were going to work out.

"I'm hungry," David called out as he shuffled from the tent.

Melinda wiped her face then put on the smile that worked like glue in tough times. She grabbed a bowl from the bag and started to fill it.

"We're having oatmeal for breakfast and I don't want any complaints. You better eat it all."

"Ugh, mom," David protested.

"Not another word."

Alistair and Charlie woke up a little later and were just as pleased as David with their breakfast choices. They grunted and groaned, but hunger was an amazing thing and even the most unappetizing food didn't stand a chance.

After eating we started to pack up things and I decided to check in on Greg. I was all for sleeping in, but if we wanted to make it to the base by nightfall we needed to get moving.

"Yo Greg," I called from outside of his tent. "Time to get up man."

When he didn't respond, I unzipped the cover and leaned in. He was lying on the floor with his sleeping bag thrown to the side. His shirt was hanging off and beads of sweat covered his skin, even though it was in the low seventies.

"Greg," I called and gave him a nudge.

He groaned and rolled over.

"Rough night?" I asked.

"You could say that."

"Well if you're up to it, I'd like to get moving."

"Yeah, give me ten."

I nodded and headed back outside. True to his word ten minutes later he was dressed and packing up. He'd pretty much drank down a bowl of oatmeal and was looking like a new man.

With our bags zipped up and food in our bellies, we left our little camp behind and started our journey into the unknown. It was funny how a new day could make everything seem better.

"It's gonna be risky crossing 41," Greg said as we pushed through the twisted branches.

"I figure we keep cover in the woods a little while longer and cross where it thins out."

Greg sniffled then shook his head in agreement. We'd only been walking for a few minutes and he was looking like he was recovering from a hangover.

"You look like shit," Melinda told him.

Shrugging, he laughed. "You're just noticing?"

"Mom can be a bit direct. She doesn't understand the meaning of subtle," Alistair said in a nonchalant tone.

"Find me a woman that does," Greg replied.

As we trudged through the woods my stress started to fade. Things almost felt normal, felt like this was something we should've been doing all along. They sky was clear, the weather was nice, all things considered, it was a good day.

My feet crunching over the dead leaves became a cadence. I fell into the rhythm and burned through the distance like I ran marathons for a living. It was easy to zone out and let my mind wander.

At times, I'd give the boys a ride on my neck. They were keen to complain about how tired they were and it was easier to carry them than deal with their whining.

"Alright, that's enough," I groaned and let David down.

He complained that he hadn't ridden long enough, but my shoulders ached. He was a dense, heavy kid and unlike Charlie, I felt every step I took with him on my neck.

For the next hour, we pushed through the clustered forest in silence. I led the way, breaking branches and clearing a path so David and Charlie could pass. Even with the cool weather it was grueling work and by midday my shirt was drenched in sweat.

107

"Time for a water break," I declared as I stared up at the sun.

We found a fallen tree and used it as a bench. The kids took a seat and gulped down an entire bottle of water each, then finished off a bag of chips. It made sense to go ahead and let them eat all of the perishable food as soon as they could. It wouldn't be long before all we had left was MRE's.

David and Charlie were doing well for the amount of distance we'd covered. I was impressed even though I'd carried them about fifty percent of the time. I already knew Alistair wouldn't have any issues. Greg on the other hand, was breathing erratically and hadn't stopped sweating since he'd woke up.

"You gonna be alright?" I asked Greg and offered him a bottle of water.

He grabbed it and poured half of it over his head. After swigging the rest, he looked up at me and shrugged. "I'm good man. Just got a bit of a fever...nothing to worry about."

"You keep saying don't worry, but you keep getting worse. It's got me worried Greg. We need to do something about your arm."

Greg stood up, I'm sure to make some over the top gesture about his great health, but he never got the chance. The sound of a woman screaming ripped through the air and I spun around.

"It's coming from the road," Greg said.

I turned to Melinda. "Stay here."

CHAPTER 13

WHAT THE WORLD HAS

BECOME

I slipped through the trees with Greg right behind me. Moving as fast as I could, without making a raucous, I clawed my way toward the shouting. The screams grew louder and louder the closer we came and whatever was happening, I could tell a great deal of pain was involved.

I stopped short of the road, where I was still covered by the thick foliage. Silently pushing the branches out of the way, I looked out to the street. There was an older, brown pick-up truck pulled off to the side, still running. A half-naked woman was scampering away while three men laughed and kicked at her.

"No, please no!" the woman shouted.

She was wearing a torn, white t-shirt and underwear. Her face was bloodied and bruised and her knees were scratched up. From what I could tell she was probably in her early thirties and had kept herself in good shape...up until now.

The men were an assortment of shady looking characters. They were all heavy set and looked in dire need of baths. One was dark-skinned with thick, curly hair and meaty hands like a construction worker. The other two looked like twin brothers. Both were beet red from the sun with brown, buzzed hair and thick, graying beards.

"What the hell?" Greg mumbled.

One of the brothers bent down and grabbed the woman's leg. He pulled her back toward the truck as she kicked and screamed hysterically.

"Not again, no! Please, please just let me go!" she yelled.

"Shut up bitch!" the man spat back.

The darker man lunged forward and smacked her across the face then grabbed her other leg. "It's my turn now Henry!" he shouted and pushed the other man away.

Flashes of Mike came to mind. The brewing guilt in my stomach started to boil and I lowered my head. I couldn't believe this was happening again.

"We have to do something," I mumbled. Although I wasn't sure what we could possibly do.

I motioned to stand up and Greg grabbed my arm.

"You're going to get us killed," he grunted.

"She's gonna get killed," I retorted.

"If you go over there and the three of them kick our ass, what do you think is gonna happen next? Huh? Do you think they won't find your little family waiting back there? Do you think Alistair will stand a chance when he tries to protect his mom? And what do you think they'll do with the little ones? Best case, they're left in the middle of the woods alone."

He painted a pretty sullen picture. A picture that I hadn't come to accept until then. Sticking your neck out, trying to play the hero would only end bad for the people you loved. I had too much to lose and I had to make sure I looked out for my family first.

But it was hard, hard to watch and even harder to swallow. I didn't even know the woman, but I knew women. She was someone's wife, someone's mother, someone's daughter. And where were the men that were supposed to protect her?

"Please stop," the woman said in a faltering voice.

The man slid between her legs and thrust himself forward. The woman grunted and cried, but had no more energy to offer any real resistance. With an animalistic grunt, he ripped her t-shirt

111

completely off then grabbed her behind the head and pulled her forward.

Kneeling there, behind the cover of trees I felt like a coward. I felt empty, like I was just as bad as the men that were raping her. I couldn't believe the world had been reduced to this in weeks. I hadn't realized how fickle the constructs that man had built were. It took nothing for them to fall apart, nothing for us to lose our morality and return to the cavemen that only knew one law, take what you can.

From behind those trees I saw the fall of humanity. I saw the end of the world and felt broken pieces of my own beliefs crumbling to sand. I saw what we were truly capable of, I saw mankind's deconstruction.

"Let's go," I whispered.

The woman had fallen silent and now the only sounds were the grunts and groans of the man entering her over and over. It was a sickening noise and I could feel the little bit of food in my stomach rumble toward my throat. With shame in my heart, I turned and headed into the forest.

Once we made it back I could see the worry written across Melinda's face. I was so happy to see her, I rushed forward and squeezed her in my arms.

"What happened?" she asked.

"Nothing," I replied and let her go. I looked her in the eyes and smiled. "Nothing to worry about."

That lie took a toll on me. I could feel physical pain as the words left my lips. That woman was most likely going to die. She'd probably be raped for days then murdered or left to the elements and I didn't even have the honor to admit that she was there.

"That was a lot of screaming for nothing to worry about," Melinda continued to press me. "Were there people out there? How many? Was everything okay?"

I looked past her and stared at Alistair then David and Charlie. Seeing their faces brought everything into perspective for me, at least I felt like it did. I'd made the right choice.

"Everybody here is safe Melinda. That's what matters. We need to get moving."

CHAPTER 14

THERE ARE ONLY HARD CHOICES

I had severely overestimated our ability to move through the twisted trees and underbrush or just how far we needed to go. We were now coming up on our fourth day in the woods and still hadn't made it to the narrow part of the highway to cross. Our water was running low and Greg looked like he needed an emergency room. I was starting to fear that the next morning he might not wake up.

"Hopefully this is our last night out here," I said as me Alistair set up the tent.

We were in a small clearing we'd made with pocket knives and elbow grease. The sun had already vanished and the dull haze remained that preceded darkness. That didn't matter much, we'd become pros at pitching a tent and I was certain we could do it blindfolded.

"Dad," Alistair started. "You've said that every night. I think we might just become permanent residents of the forest, woodland creatures."

I laughed and shook my head. It was good to see some of his sense of humor had survived all of this. I often times sat up at night wondering just how much of his innocence would be lost, before we found some kind of normalcy.

After a quick dinner and what we considered a ration-sized bit of water we tucked in for the night. David and Charlie were starting to get used to the tent life and we're taking up much more room than was needed. It didn't really bother me that much though, I liked keeping them close.

The next morning, we woke up early, hoping to cross the highway before the sun was fully up. I knew we were close and moving through the fog at dawn was probably the safest way to travel.

While Melinda fed the kids breakfast, I handled the unpleasant task of waking up Greg. He had a thing about being disturbed and normally met intruders with whatever item was in arm's reach. The last morning I caught a boot to the side of my face for my troubles.

"Greg," I called from the front of his tent. "Time to hit it."

I waited a few moments for an answer. When he didn't reply, I poked my head inside then entered.

"Greg."

A low moan was his response. With barely any light, I felt my way toward him and found him stretched out across the floor. His lips were cracked and chap and his skin was icy to the touch although he was covered in sweat.

"Greg...Greg can you hear me?"

His chest barely rose and fell as if he could hardly draw breath. Reaching across the floor, I grabbed his bag and pulled out a water bottle and a rag. I wet it then wiped it across his face and tipped some of the water into his mouth. He gagged and the water trickled down the side of his cheek.

"Don't you do this Greg," I grumbled. "Not now."

His eyes were glossed over and he seemed to be staring at nothing. His mouth was cracked and he exhaled a weak, shallow breath every few seconds.

I reached across him and pulled back the bandage that he'd wrapped around his shoulder. The smell alone almost made me vomit. The wound was nearly black with crusted puss and swollen skin surrounding it. It looked like it belonged on a corpse.

"Greg what the fuck!" I snapped at him. "I told you this needed to be looked at. I told you it would get infected."

He didn't respond. If anything, his breathing slowed a little.

"You have to clean this. You hear me? Fuck! I'll be back."

I turned around and headed for the door. As I stepped out Alistair almost ran me over and from the look in his eyes, I knew something was wrong.

"Someone's coming!" he said urgently.

I rushed toward Melinda and she'd already started packing up things and getting the boys ready to move.

"That way," she pointed. "I don't know how far, but I could hear them talking when I was throwing out trash."

I tried to hide my expression, but Melinda knew me too well. My face said it all and she started to press me for answers.

"What's going on?" she asked. "Who are they?"

"I don't know."

"Randall..."

"I don't know," I replied. "They could be the guys from the road the other day."

"You said that was nothing"

"Just...just stay with the kids...be ready to go," I said then grabbed the pistol from my bag and headed deeper into the woods.

I followed the direction she pointed in and I could hear faint voices after only a few steps. After about fifty yards I stopped and stooped down. A group of five men with rifles were barreling through the forest, not worried about hiding themselves. They moved quickly, but clumsily through the branches and twisted vines.

With a deep breath, I moved a bit closer, hoping to make out what they were talking about. I army crawled across the leaf-covered floor then tucked myself behind a patch of palmetto bushes.

"You really think they've survived out here for this long," one of the men said. He was dressed in hunting fatigues and wearing a red hat.

"They had food, they had water. They could live out here. We need to find them," another man declared angrily. "If we don't, we ain't gonna survive out here."

I could feel my heart jump. "Fuck!" I grumbled.

As quickly as I could without making a sound, I ran back to our little camp. Melinda had a terrified look on her face and she had every reason to.

"It's the guys from the neighborhood. They're looking for us," I told her.

"What? Why?"

"I don't know, but we have to go now."

"What about Greg."

I'd been waiting for that question and I still didn't have a good answer. Greg needed a doctor or he was going to die. There was no way around that. And there was no doctor.

"Take the boys and head that way," I pointed. "I'll get Greg. Go, and be fast...I'll catch up!"

For once in her life, Melinda didn't question me. She gave me a kiss then grabbed Charlie and David by the hand and led them off in the opposite direction.

Alistair hung back for a second. I smiled at him and patted him on the shoulder.

"I'll catch up, I promise. You keep your mom and brothers safe."

He gave me a skeptical look.

"I'll catch up!" I reiterated.

He nodded and then gave me a hug. I hugged him back and told him I loved him. He said the same and then with a pained face, he ran after Melinda.

Sighing, I headed back into Greg's tent. This was a moment that I'd be fearing for the last few days. The moment when he'd no longer be able to keep up with us and I'd be forced to make a decision. Him or my family.

I'd hoped the decision would come much later, but as fate would have it, my hand was forced.

"Greg," I called. "Greg, bad guys are coming. They want to hurt us and we can't stay here. We have to move fast, but I can't carry you and keep my family safe."

I paused and took another long, deep breath. "If you can move...if you can move at all, say something now."

He didn't respond. Just the same slow, shallow breathing. It sounded like a can rattling around on an empty street. It sounded like the whispers of death.

Why was I always here? Was it my sentence to be a witness to people dying until my time had finally come? What had I done to deserve this?

It sounded insane to even question it. Why complain when I was still here? Why should I pity myself when others had lost their lives? But I knew why, there were things worse than death and one of those things was seeing death all around you and not being able to stop it. I didn't want to be around death any longer.

"Greg," I called again with more desperation in my voice.

A harsh exhalation was his reply and it chilled my bones. Greg was gone, his body just didn't know it yet. He would join the growing list of unfortunate souls whose paths had crossed mine.

I stared at his pale face with sadness in my heart. He'd sacrificed his life for my family. If it wasn't for him we'd be dead. And now here he was, taking his last breaths in the middle of a forest.

I probably would've stayed there a little longer and gave him more chances, but I heard breaking branches and rustling leaves. Then I heard the men's voices. My decision had been made.

I grabbed Greg's bag and gave him one last look. Then grunting, I turned and rushed out of the tent and left him behind to die.

CHAPTER 15

ONE FOOT FORWARD

I ran through the twisted branches as fast as I could. In my panic to get my family away I hadn't thought about how you could get lost just ten feet into the tangled forest. Now, I had no idea where they were and even less of an idea on how I was going to find them.

I fought against the urge to yell for them. I knew the men had to be close and that made me think of Greg.

What would they do to him once they found him? Was he already dead? The guilt was starting to slow me down. I'd not only left him to die, but to get tortured and murdered.

The sun had started to rise and burn off the fog from the forest floor. My visibility improved, but all I could see were the gnarled branches of oak trees.

After nearly ten minutes of running I slowed down and leaned against a massive tree. I took some water out of my bag and gulped it down then wiped my face with the back of my hand. I looked around the wooded maze for signs, for any trace of where my family might be.

"Come on guys," I mumbled to myself.

With a deep breath, I straightened up. I adjusted my bag then took off at a jog the same direction I'd been going.

I ran for several minutes until the trees started to thin. The naked branches faded and the sky came through like a game of peek-a-boo.

Slowing down, I came to a stop in a clearing and stared to the heavens. It was a dull winter day, with long, drab clouds floating across a gray background. The sun was hidden behind the murky, swirls of sky and a single black bird sailed overhead.

A cool wind shook the skinny branches above me. They rustled together, making an ominous noise. I squinted and stared at them, completely missing the sound of footsteps coming up behind me.

"Don't move!" a man suddenly shouted.

I paused and felt my heart crawl into my throat. A million different thoughts rushed through my mind and my head swam in confusion. I should've known the dangers of my new reality were always there, always waiting to catch me with my guard down.

"I don't want any trouble," I replied. "I'm just lo..."

"Shut up!" the man snapped.

I felt the barrel of a rifle push against the back of my skull. The icy, rigid metal tickled like death and froze my insides.

"Don't you move," he said again and pushed the rifle harder.

Clenching my fists, I waited in silence, wondering what would come next. Did he just want my stuff? Were there more people out there or would he just shoot me and leave me to die? I couldn't let that happen. Melinda and the kids needed me and somehow, I had to make it back to them.

"What do you want?" I asked.

He jabbed me again with the rifle and I grunted. Right then, I decided if I was gonna die, it wasn't going to be with some asshole shooting me in the back. If I was gonna die, I planned to put up one hell of a fight.

Moving slightly, I slid my hand up my leg and wrapped my fingers around the pistol I had tucked in my waistband. I immediately felt a sense of power and grinned at the poor bastard's stupidity of thinking he was the only one armed.

"What the hell are you doing out here?" he snarled.

"Same as you idiot," I said sharply.

I could hear him adjusting his grip on the gun and I seized the opportunity. Spinning around, I brought one hand across the barrel and smacked the rifle to the side. My other hand withdrew my pistol and I leveled it at the man's head.

"Don't move!" I growled.

The man paused and stared at me defiantly. He seemed to be measuring me, wondering if he could get away with charging the few steps and taking me to the ground. Wondering if I was the type to shoot and ask questions later or if I'd freeze at the moment when it mattered.

He was a dark-skinned guy with a nearly bald head. He had a hefty build, about six feet tall and his ashy fingers trembled as they clenched the rifle that hung at his side. That's when I realized, he was just as frightened as I was.

"Who are you?" I asked in the roughest voice I could manage.

He didn't respond. He just glared at me and tightened his jaw over and over. I stared back at him and wondered if my pistol was even loaded. Stupid mistakes were gonna be the death of me and the fact that I sucked at operating a firearm was at the top of the list.

A branch snapped somewhere in the distance and I took my eyes off of him for a split second. When I looked back, he was pointing the rifle at me with a stupid smirk on his face. Now we were both in mortal danger, but he looked like he knew how to use his rifle and I wasn't even sure mine would fire.

"Koran stop! That's my husband!" I heard Melinda's voice shout.

"What?" we both said in unison and slightly lowered our guns.

"Randall," Melinda said as she rushed to my side.

With one hand, I grabbed her around the waist. With the other, I kept my gun pointing at Koran...or whatever the hell his name was.

"Who the hell are you?"

"Babe," Melinda whispered and I felt her hand touch the side of my face. "He's okay, he...he helped us. Him and his wife have a camp, the kids are there."

I huffed and continued to grill the man with a stern face. If I'd learned anything in my short time in the apocalypse, it was that trust had to be earned.

"Where are you from?" I asked suspiciously. "You live around here?"

"Symphony Isles. You?"

I didn't reply. I was still trying to decide how trustworthy he was. "What street do you live on?"

He scoffed. "3271 Mariners Cove. I'm sure there a few vacancies now, if you're looking."

"The kids are waiting," Melinda said.

Grinning, I tucked my gun back into my pants and extended my hand. "My name's Randall."

"Koran Meyers," he said and shook my hand.

I followed them back to Koran's camp where everyone else was waiting. Alistair jumped up and ran to give me a hug followed by David and Charlie.

"Told you I'd catch up," I said and patted him on the shoulder.

"Randall, this is Stephanie. Stephanie, this is Randall," Koran said as he introduced me to his wife.

She was a thin, short lady with braided hair and a soft face. She wore glasses and had a machete strapped to her belt loop. Her t-shirt was ripped and her beige pants were tucked into her boots like she was going mountain hiking.

Standing next to her, was a young girl about the same age as Alistair. She had a confused look on her face and I was sure she was having as tough a time with things as the rest of the kids were.

"This is my daughter Ashley," Koran said.

I shook her hand then turned back to Koran. "How long have you guys been out here?"

They had one large tent set up in the middle of the clearing. Around the perimeter, they had a string tied to each tree with bells hanging from it. A clothes line spanned between two branches and they'd dug a fire pit that they'd obviously been using to burn trash.

"Too long," he replied.

"Well, there's some guys headed this way. They're not the kind you want to mess around with. You won't be safe here much longer."

"Where's Greg," Melinda suddenly asked.

I lowered my eyes and shook my head from side to side. "He didn't make it," I replied. "Alistair, help your brothers get their bags. We have to get moving."

Melinda looked at me and sighed. I tried to avoid her eyes, my own guilt at what I had done was enough to deal with. I didn't need her judging me too.

"Wait...where are you guys heading?" Koran asked desperately.

"Far away from here," I said. I didn't want to give him too much information and I was in a hurry to separate myself from them.

"The marina," Melinda blurted out. "We're gonna take a sail boat."

I shot her an angry look and she shrugged.

"That...that's a good idea," Koran responded. "Mind if we tag along?"

I swallowed and bit my bottom lip. Huffing, I glanced at Melinda again and cursed her with my eyes.

"I can help," Koran said. "I know a few things about survival and, and I can sail."

I groaned. He'd brought up the one thing that would make me give him any consideration at all. I stared at him and knew that I was gonna regret the decision I was about to make.

"Fine, but we have to go now," I replied.

Koran smiled. "Stephanie, Ashley, time to pack up," he said and started collecting his things.

I watched him walk away then turned to Melinda and pulled her to the side. "What is wrong with you?"

"What?" she said a little too loudly.

I cast a hesitant glance in Koran's direction then continued. "We don't know this guy. What are you thinking telling him where we are going? We can't trust anyone?"

"I'm sorry...but you heard him. He can sail, we need someone that can sail."

I sighed. "I hope you're right Melinda. Cause if this turns out bad, you put all the kids in jeopardy."

CHAPTER 16

NOT OUT OF THE WOODS

"So, what's your story Koran?" I asked as we walked through the thinning trees.

I could see the road about half a mile ahead of us and the smell of salt water was starting to reach my nose. The changing scenery spurred me to walk a little faster and I felt hopeful for the first time.

"What do you mean?" Koran replied.

"How'd you end up out here.? What's your deal?"

Koran laughed. "You guys have those, those gangs in your neighborhood?"

"Gangs?"

"Yeah, the guys with guns and shit, taking people's stuff. Killing anyone that stood up to them."

"Yeah, we got out the day they showed up."

"Well, we weren't so lucky," he said then paused.

He stared down at the ground like his mind had drifted somewhere else and for the next few yards we walked in silence. I'd seen my fair share of horrors so I didn't press him. Reliving the nightmares of the last several weeks wasn't an easy task.

"They came early on, maybe twenty or so," he started again. "Killed...killed lots of folk. A couple of us...families, hid in a foreclosed house at the back of the neighborhood. We lasted for a week, then the national guard showed up."

"Yeah, they came to our neighborhood too," I added.

He half-smiled. "Well, the gangs were armed to the teeth and they weren't about to give up the neighborhood without a fight. I mean the place is gated with one narrow street in and nothing but the bay behind us. It got ugly and the fight spilled to the back of the neighborhood. We lost ten trying to get out before they bombed the place to shit."

"Bombed it?" I asked in shock.

"Yeah, guess they got their hands on some mortars. Symphony Isles is gone."

He stopped talking then looked up ahead and nodded. We were feet from the roadway and I could see the cluster of thinning mangroves that bordered the marina.

"Well, those are some of the guys that were back there, the ones following us. I guess they've been after us since we left the neighborhood."

"Be happy you didn't have to deal with them," he replied coldly.

"Melinda," I called back. "We're close."

She came to a stop beside me and smiled. Her arm wrapped around mine and she leaned her head onto my shoulder.

David and Charlie were tagging along behind her. Alistair was dragging ass, bringing up the rear, talking with Ashley. They'd taken to each other, probably figured they were the last teenagers alive.

I crouched down and looked across the road. "Have you seen any other people?" I asked.

"Not really, not since we left. We've tried to avoid people best we can, you know?"

I knew. "It's odd though. Where the hell is everyone?"

"Evacuated," he replied.

"Evacuated?"

"Yeah...you didn't hear?"

"Honey," Stephanie interrupted him. "This can wait. We should get to the other side, back to the cover of the trees."

She was right. The forest had thinned to stubs and we were out in the open. The memory of Mike or Greg, or that poor woman on the side of the road was not far from my mind. This wasn't a good place to be.

"Alistair, hurry up," I shouted to him.

He waved his hand at me and went back to talking with Ashley. I started toward them when a crackle sent us all diving to the ground. Panic and fear rushed through my body and I realized, we'd lingered too long.

From my stomach, I looked up and stared back in the direction we'd just come. I couldn't see anyone yet, but I could hear them back there.

Another shot rang through the air followed by several more. Dirt and leaves jumped to life as the speeding metal missed its intended target. A bullet smashed into the ground a few feet away and sprinkles of soil showered my face.

"Run!" I yelled to Melinda.

Pushing past my fear, I forced myself to stand. Alistair was a few yards away, pulling at Ashley's arm, trying to force her to run. Melinda and the boys were already crossing the street and Koran and Stephanie looked torn between leaving their daughter behind and risking their lives to save her.

"Alistair come on!" I yelled as I ran toward the gunfire.

I could see flashes of the men's clothes between the twisted tree trunks. They were closing in and pretty soon their wild shots would find their mark. They obviously weren't that skilled with a rifle, but they only needed to be lucky.

"We have to go. We have to go now!" I yelled.

"She twisted her leg dad. She can't run," Alistair replied.

Ashley groaned and pulled her leg to her chest. She was wearing a pair of low-top tennis shoes and I could already see the swelling in her ankle.

"Look, you help her across the street and I'll distract them. Tell your mom to get to the marina and I'll meet you guys there."

"Dad, we can both carry her," Alistair replied.

"Don't argue with me. Just take her."

I helped Ashley up and she wrapped her arm around Alistair's shoulder. Alistair frowned at me, but I didn't have time to keep explaining myself.

"Go!" I shouted.

With that, I ran back toward the group of men, hoping I didn't get shot for my troubles. "Hey assholes!" I yelled and streaked off to the side.

The hiss of gunfire was my answer, my plan was working. I could hear branches snapping to my right and more gunshots rang out. I ducked my head as I headed deeper into the trees.

Still running at full speed I pulled the black handgun from my waistband. I took a few more strides then hid behind a cluster of oaks and froze.

I tried to calm my breathing as my lungs begged for air. My hands trembled and I cursed myself for trying to play the hero yet again. Koran and his family didn't deserve my help, he'd left us to die, he'd even left his own daughter to die.

"He went this way," someone whispered.

I could hear several footsteps and I knew they were close. Now, all I needed was a few moments of courage. A few moments of insanity that would allow me to do what needed to be done.

The sound of crunching leaves rustled a few feet away. I slowly leaned to my left and peaked around the side of the tree. All five of the men were together, they were only a few yards away, heading in my direction.

Cautiously, I circled around the trunk as they got closer. They walked right past me and I stepped out behind them.

"Freeze!" I yelled and with shaky hands pointed my gun at their backs. "Don't turn around. Drop your guns!"

"Hey now fella, we're just out here surviving like the rest of you," one of the men replied.

He was wearing a red and black flannel jacket and a beanie cap on his head. His denim jeans were covered in dirt and what looked like dried blood. I hoped it belonged to some animal, but from the stories Koran told, I knew that wasn't the case.

The rest of the men were in camo like they'd been hunting deer or something. They looked like the outdoorsy type. Much better suited for the forest than I was, even though they'd proven that they couldn't shoot for shit.

"I said drop the fucking guns!" I shouted again.

Like a snare drum their rifles rattled to the ground. They raised their hands slightly and then the man in the jacket slowly started to turn around.

"Calm down now. We don't want anyone getting hurt," he said.

I glared at him, trying my hardest to look menacing. My arms shook violently and I thought I'd either drop the gun or accidentally shoot him.

"What do you guys want? Why are you following us?"

"Where are the rest of your people?" he asked and took a step toward me.

I jabbed the gun out and rocked backward. "I said don't move. I'll fucking shoot you, I mean it."

"Parker...you're gonna get us killed," one of the other men said. He was wearing fatigues and a red hat. Out of all of them, he looked like he wanted to be there the least.

"He don't wanna kill anybody. Ain't that right?" Parker said.

"I'll shoot you, I swear to God I will," I snapped at him.

"Whoa...take it easy man," he said lowly, but kept moving forward.

I stepped back again and stumbled a bit on the root of a tree. Parker lunged at me as I recovered. I jumped back just out of his reach and squeezed the trigger.

He grunted and crouched to the floor with closed eyes and clenched his fists. But instead of a gunshot I was only greeted with an empty clicking sound.

Parker opened his eyes and glared at me in surprise. I pulled the trigger again with the same result. Then again and again. Fear choked me and my breath got stuck in my throat.

Parker straightened up and smiled from ear to ear. Laughing, he said, "You even load that thing? You even know how?"

135

I looked down at the gun with a confused face. I'd put too much faith in a piece of useless metal.

Parker smacked the gun from my hand and brought his fist crashing against my temple. Disorientated, I staggered then fell back on my ass. I blinked wildly and stars exploded in front of my eyes. It felt like my head bad been slammed in between a door.

"You in trouble now," one of them said and they all started to laugh.

Their cackling hoots and jeers sounded like a swarm of bees. A swarm of killer bees, zipping around in excitement before they delivered a swift and painful death.

Someone moved closer and stopped. With blurry vision, I tried to make out the figure standing over me. Their face came within inches of mine and they started to speak.

"We're gonna find the rest of your party," Parker's voice said deliberately. "That woman...we're gonna fuck her good. Probably keep her around for a while. Til we get tired of her, then who knows? The rest of em we're gonna kill slow, real slow," he finished in a low raspy voice.

"No! Please no!" I pleaded.

CHAPTER 17

MARCH TO THE MARINA

I begged Parker to let me go. I offered him everything I could think of, but he was an evil, vile bastard. His entire group didn't want anything more than to cause destruction and pain wherever they went.

"Whatever you got, we're just gonna take. Ain't no sense in bargaining with a dead man," Parker said.

"Please, just let me go. You don't have to kill me, you don't need to."

"Hell, we want to. This is what we do boy. Don't nobody ever have to kill, but it sure as shit feels good."

Parker started to laugh then a hiss sizzled the air and ended with a thud. His heckling fell silent and something splattered all over my face. Blinking, I wiped at my eyes and realized it was blood and brain fragments.

"What the fuck?" the rest of the men started to shout in unison.

They quickly grabbed their rifles from the ground, but before they could even raise them two more hisses whizzed through the air and two more bodies fell.

"Shit...holy shit!" one of the other men yelled as he spun around with no plan.

My head was still swarming, but I managed to stand and attempted to collect my bearings. There was a large tree to my right and I awkwardly stumbled to it. I fell against the raspy bark then looked back to toward the rest of Parker's friends.

There were only two left and they were turning from side to side trying to find the source of the gunfire. One of them stopped and looked at me. His face was gaunt and his eyes trembled with confusion.

"Where the fuck are they?" he asked and pointed his rifle.

Before I could respond two crackles erupted in my ears and both men fell dead. I breathed a sigh of relief before I realized, whoever was doing the shooting might be shooting at me as well.

Grunting, I dropped to the ground and didn't move. I waited quietly, hoping my silence would keep me hidden. Minutes ticked by and I thought I might be in the clear, until I heard a footfall and a twig snapped a few feet away.

"You can get up now," a voice called.

I lifted my head and braced myself. With clenched teeth, I pushed up to all fours and opened my eyes. Koran was standing in front of me with a half grin on his face.

"Jesus," I said and huffed, blowing out what felt like years of anxiety. "I thought you left."

"Nah, just had to get the ladies and the kids tucked in first."

"Who the fuck are you?" I asked and looked around at the scattered dead bodies.

He shrugged and offered me his hand. "Come on, we gotta get to the marina."

I took his hand and stood up then dusted off my pants. Koran walked off then grabbed my handgun from the dirt and held it out to me. I took it and reluctantly tucked it back into my pants.

"I can help you with that if you want. You know teach you to use it...you're gonna need it."

"Sure," I replied.

"Are you good to move? The others should be at the marina by now."

I nodded and we took off toward the road. He kept the pace slow at first, he was watching me cautiously. I guess he thought the blow to my head was worse than I let on.

I felt fine, but who knew how long that would last. I'd been doing more physical activity in the last month that I had in the last ten years of my life.

"What were you talking about earlier?" I asked as we walked across the road and headed toward the mangroves.

"About what?"

"Evacuations."

"Oh, that. As far as I know all of Hillsborough County was evacuated. The storm surge was supposed to be over twenty feet out here."

"So, what the hell happened?"

"The power outage, well the EMP. Things got dropped, signals got crossed and a few neighborhoods out here never got the memo. That's why the national guard came. I don't know what happened in your neighborhood, but they came to evacuate us."

I didn't immediately respond. I let his words sink in as I tried to make sense of what I'd seen and what he was telling me.

"They're just around the bend," he said and pointed. "Your family."

"Thanks," I replied.

He nodded.

"I mean for everything. For back there with...you know. Thanks. I didn't think I was gonna see my family again."

"Don't mention it."

"So how do you know all of that? How do you know it was an EMP?"

"I used to be military."

"That makes sense."

Koran laughed. "Nah, not like that. I mean, I was Navy. Handled communications systems on a ship, but they taught me how to shoot and a few things about surviving outdoors."

"You said you used to be military."

"Yeah, I'm a contractor at the base now. Well I guess I was a contractor at the base. The day all of this shit started I was at work. I shouldn't really be telling you this, but I guess it doesn't matter now anyway. That crazy lightning storm that happened set off CHAMP."

"CHAMP?"

"Yeah, it's a non-nuclear EMP system, the Air force has been working on with Boeing."

"That shit is real?"

"Yeah, still in the testing phases, but the storm set it off. Not everything was impacted, but being we're so close to the base we got the brunt of it."

"That's crazy," I said and rubbed my hands across my face.

"There they are," Koran pointed.

We'd made it to the nature preserve that ended at the marina. Melinda, Stephanie and the kids were sitting on a bench facing the water. Alistair and Ashley were a few yards away, having what looked like a serious discussion.

"Looks like a few boats survived the storm. We're in luck," Koran said.

I took a deep breath, then headed toward my family. "Melinda," I called.

She stood up and turned around. A smile spread over her face and she waved. I waved back then suddenly felt the Earth shift beneath my feet.

The sensation was unfamiliar. I felt like I was standing on a beach ball trying to balance myself. Like I was walking on a treadmill that was on top of a merry-go-round inside of a crashing airplane.

"What the hell is going on?" Koran shouted.

To our left the ground split open and a stream of searing hot gas belted into the air. Ahead of us the water in the bay started to whip from left to right, crashing up against the dock, sending a salty mist toward the sky.

A loud grumbling echoed in my ears and I fought to stay upright. Every step I took toward my family seemed futile, the ground crackled and splintered, sending me stumbling backwards. The loose sand shifted and became a conveyor belt of death as the Earth swallowed everything that fell into the cracks.

Watching the floor rip apart, Steve suddenly came to mind. This couldn't be happening, but it was. I was watching it with my own eyes and I still couldn't believe it. He had been right all along and I'd dismissed him. But I couldn't deny it now.

"Earthquake!" I screamed at the top of my lungs.

CHAPTER 18

WE WILL SURVIVE

I'd never felt so helpless in my life. They were right there, close enough to throw something at, but I couldn't make it to them. My family needed me and the very Earth was trying to tear us apart.

"I'm coming," I yelled.

Melinda looked mortified. Tears streamed from her eyes as she grabbed the kids and tried to balance across the shaky boardwalk.

I leapt over cracks in the ground, recklessly trying to make my way toward them. Every time I got closer the ground would splinter and crack, sending me in a different direction.

With a loud snap, half of the dock cracked in half and plunged into the water. Melinda let out a shrilling yelp and ran toward the rocks on the far side. More of the dock split apart and disappeared beneath the churning tide.

Then as sudden as it started, the shaking stopped. The ground grew still and the buckled sheets of rock came to rest on one another.

I gathered myself for a moment and stared around in shock. The marina looked like a warzone, smoke plumed from giant fissures and boat debris stuck up from the sand like blades of grass.

But all was still, so without a second thought, I rushed toward Melinda and the kids.

"Are you okay?" I asked as I grabbed her by the shoulders.

"I'm...I'm fine."

I looked at the kids and gave them each a hug. David and Charlie had wild looks on their faces, but they were unharmed. Alistair looked more amazed than anything else and Ashley stared off toward the water.

"I guess we do have earthquakes now," Alistair said with a grin.

I shook my head at him and cut my eyes.

"Ashley," Stephanie cried out as she pulled her daughter into her arms.

Ashley scoffed and let out a grunting noise. Koran stopped at their side and wrapped his arms around the both of them.

"I thought I was going to lose you guys," he said.

I looked around at the fractured landscape. Giant cracks and crevices riddled the ground like scars. The sidewalk was warped and at places pushed together so the concrete rose into the air like a tent. It was hard to believe we'd been in the middle of it all and were still alive.

The bay had calmed down, but the marina was trashed. Boats that were previously tied to the dock had been ripped away and crushed. Many of them were slammed into the seawall and were now slowly sinking.

"It was just a tremor," Koran said.

"We almost died," I retorted. "That wasn't **just** anything. We need to get out of here."

"Well, your sailing plan might be out of the window."

I looked around at all of the demolished boats and sulked. "Not sure we want to be on the water after that anyway."

Koran laughed. "I don't want to be on the land."

"Dad!" Alistair called.

He'd walked down the remainder of the boardwalk and was staring out into the water. He waved his hand at me and then pointed at something nearly half a mile out.

"Will that work?"

Out in the water, floating like a beacon of hope was a thirty-foot catamaran. It was white with blue stripes down the hull and bright yellow sails. A small motorboat was tied behind it and bobbed gently in the swaying water.

"I'll be damned," Koran said excitedly.

"Can you sail that thing?"

"Oh yeah. I can sail that."

I smiled and felt a bit of relief then realized, we still had to get the boat. Staring into the gray water, I frowned and looked back at Koran.

"We're gonna have to swim to it."

"Yeah, I'd figured that much. You okay with that?"

I nodded. I wasn't sure I had a choice, my limited sailing experience told me it would take at least two of us to get the boat moving.

I turned my head and gazed back at the demolished marina. My eyes rested on a small building that had buckled and caved in on itself. It was possibly moments from collapsing to the ground completely. "Fuck," I grumbled.

"What is it?" Koran asked.

"The guard station," I groaned and pointed at the crumbling remains. "The keys to our plan are in there."

"Shit," Koran replied. "I'd really like to get out of here before something else happens."

"I'll take Alistair and try to find the keys."

"Okay, I'll see what I can scavenge from the boats. We're gonna need gas to motor back to pick up everyone."

"What about us?" Melinda asked.

"Ashley can stay with the kids," Koran said. "You two can help search for supplies."

"Be careful," I added. "If it looks too dangerous just leave it. I don't need you falling into one of these trenches."

Melinda smiled and I gave her a kiss on the forehead. I turned to Alistair and raised my eyebrows. "You ready big guy?"

He shrugged which was about as optimistic as he got these days. I took it as a good sign he didn't outright refuse to join me on my treasure hunt.

"Alright, I'll start with the boats that haven't sunk. Let's hurry up, the weather isn't looking too promising," Koran said then headed off.

With Alistair following, I cautiously made my way toward the guard station. A lamp post that once stood next to it had been knocked over by the earthquake. It smashed through the roof and flattened part of the rickety structure like matchsticks.

"How do we know which keys belong to which boat?" Alistair asked.

I grinned. "We won't, but they were doing renovations over here for the park. Only ten or so boats were being kept here. So we'll just take them all. The hard part is gonna be getting to the keys."

I bent down and tried to lift a panel of boards that had once been the wall to the station. Straining, I pulled as hard as I could but it didn't budge.

"You could've helped," I said and cast a glance at Alistair.

"Dad, all of us together couldn't lift that. But I think I can fit in that gap."

The way the station fell, two of the walls collapsed on one another, creating a little tunnel to what remained inside. The problem was it looked like it was all going to come crashing down at any minute.

"Yeah, that's not a good idea Alistair. If you get in there and it falls over, there's no way for us to get you out."

"Well, you can't fit and it looks like that's our only way in. So, it's that or stay here dad and I don't want to stay here."

I groaned and took a deep breath. He was right, but I still didn't like the idea. With my foot, I pushed against the outside wall and it seemed to hold. If he was quick, he might just survive.

I looked up to the darkening sky. Thick, black clouds were starting to collect over our heads and I realized the weather may keep us here longer than we wanted anyway.

"Alright, hurry up. If you don't immediately see the keys, get out of there and we'll try something else."

"I'll be fine dad," Alistair replied.

He dropped to all fours then stuck his head into the little gap between the propped-up walls. Army crawling, he slid forward like a snake until only his feet were sticking out.

"You okay?" I asked.

"Yeah just had to move a few things," he called back.

Seconds later, he vanished inside and I could hear things rustling around. I balled my fists together, trying to fight off my anxiety. Every passing second felt like an eternity.

"Dad!" he suddenly shouted.

148

I jumped out of my skin then dove to the ground and crammed my head into the narrow gap. A box met my face and I stopped.

"Take this," he said as he tried to shove some supplies back through the hole.

With a breath of relief, I straightened up and pulled the box out. It was stuffed with flares, a pair of binoculars and two black and yellow radios.

"What about the keys?" I called to him. "Just get those and get out."

"But there's tons of stuff in here dad," he called back and pushed another box out.

This one had waterproof coats in it, a parka and a few life preservers. I couldn't lie, we probably needed everything that was in there, but the guard station wasn't gonna stay propped up like that forever.

"That's enough Alistair. Come on out."

"Okay, okay. I got all the keys."

I could hear him moving around to crawl back through the opening. Suddenly, the ground started to shift again. I lost my footing and fell back, rolling over a pile of rocks.

The tremor lasted only seconds, but in that time the light pole slid further down the roof and the entire building collapsed.

"No!" I shouted as a gust of sand and debris pelted me in the face.

I jumped to my feet and ran forward yelling. "Alistair! Alistair!"

A cloud of dust hung in the air and I swiped my hands wildly, trying to fan it away. Once it finally cleared I saw Alistair's legs sticking out from the pile of rubble that was once the guard station.

"Oh my God!" I groaned in pain.

But before I took another step he pulled his head out and rolled over. With a smile, he stood up and brandished a handful of keys hanging on multi-colored, floating key chains.

"I got em all," he laughed.

"Are you insane? You almost died."

"I'm fine dad. Let's go."

I looked at him for a moment and repressed the urge to smack him in the back of the head. Grunting, I snatched the keys from him then headed back toward the pier.

"You guys okay?" Melinda asked as we approached. "I thought I heard you screaming."

"It was nothing," Alistair quickly answered.

I gave him a dirty look then turned back to Melinda. "You find anything?"

"Some clothes, couple of pockets knives and a few gas cans."

"Same here," Koran added.

With our scavenging complete, we gathered everything on the pier. It was a nice-sized pile of treasure. Probably would've been more if the place hadn't been destroyed minutes earlier.

Sighing, I dropped my hiking bag and sat down at the edge of one of the planks. I started to untie my shoes and looked back to Koran.

"So how are we gonna do this?" I asked.

"Well, we swim out, climb aboard and drive the boat back here," he replied then smiled.

"That easy huh?"

"Yeah...it really is. I'm gonna take one of those plastic gas containers with me just in case the tank is empty. But with it being in the marina it should be full."

"Here," I said and handed him five of the keys. "No sense in one person having them all."

"We'll be fine," he replied as he stuffed them into his underwear.

I pulled my pants off and laid them in a pile with my shirt and shoes. The cold air sent goose bumps up and down my arms and I stared down at the water and shivered.

"How cold do you think it is?"

"Sixties maybe. Swim fast and you'll be fine."

"Yeah, swim fast," I echoed.

The water splashed up against the dock and salt sprayed my face. I shuddered and regretted the entire idea of getting a boat.

"Damn it!" Koran groaned.

I followed his eyes out into the water. The sailboat was nearly a mile away now. What we hadn't noticed was the wind and the outgoing tide. It'd be great for sailing, but we needed to get the boat first.

"Let's go now," Koran said. "It's only gonna get further away."

With that, he jumped into the water and started to breaststroke through the waves like Michael Phelps. I groaned and hesitated for a moment. A half mile swim was pushing it and now it was almost twice that, but like he said it was only getting further away.

"Wish me luck," I said and winked at Melinda.

She smiled and blew me a kiss as I dove into the frigid water. It hit me like a block of ice. Either Koran was crazy or sixty degrees was much colder than I imagined. Either way, the shock on my body was like being electrocuted.

I seized up as I sunk into the murky depths. My mind forgot everything, including what water was and that I couldn't breathe it. At least a gallon of the sea found its way down my throat. I choked and flailed my arms helplessly.

The sensation of drowning finally awoke my senses and I kicked my legs with desperation. I could feel the cold darkness pulling at my toes. Every thrust pushed me further away and closer to life.

As I broke the surface, expecting a lungful of air, a wave smashed into me and pushed me back under. At that point I lost all logic and panic took over.

I ineffectively clawed at the water as an undercurrent pulled me down. More of the icy salt-wash found its way into my mouth and my vision darkened. I gagged and swallowed the sea in an attempt to drink my way out of the ocean. But I couldn't escape the reality of what was happening.

I was going to die. I'd overestimated myself and now I'd pay with my life. The cold water was swallowing me down and every attempt I made seemed useless.

My head broke the surface again momentarily. I managed to take a quick breath before a piece of the broken dock slammed into the side of my face. I felt a sharp pain and an intense icy, burn. Then the blackness consumed me.

CHAPTER 19

BETWEEN THE DEVIL
AND THE DEEP BLUE SEA

I don't know how long I was unconscious, but I awoke to cold and darkness. My head bobbed around and I realized I was still in the sea.

Frozen hands gripped my shoulder and pulled me across the churning surface. I sucked in cold air and coughed out the salty death. With every breath, my head cleared a little more and life returned to my limbs.

I felt my feet brush up against a cluster of rocks. Jagged barnacles clawed at my skin, claiming their own piece of me. As we moved further up, the water released me and under my own weight I collapsed.

"Can you stand up?" a voice asked.

"Alistair?" I said in surprise and wiped my face and tried to focus.

"You almost drowned," he replied in a serious tone.

"Randall!" Melinda shouted as she rushed to the edge of the shore.

I stood up and started to climb up the rocks to the beach above. Alistair kept a close eye on me, following me with every step. Once I reached the top I flopped and rolled onto my back.

"Are you okay?" Melinda asked and dropped down next to me.

My head bellowed in pain, but that was superficial. I stared up at the swirling, gray sky and felt another sensation that I wasn't familiar with. A sensation that had nothing to do with my physical injuries.

"I'm okay," I replied with a scratchy voice.

"That gash looks really bad," Stephanie declared. "It's gonna need stitches."

I looked at her and nodded. With a deep breath, I sat up then nausea hit me like a semi truck. Leaning to the side, I gagged then puked up a shower of salt water.

Melinda patted my back and whispered "it's okay," in my ear. But I knew it wasn't okay. I dropped my head and let my face crash into the sand.

Lurching forward, more water spewed from my icy lips. I gagged and hacked up the ocean. My stomach twisted in pain, straining and contorting with every convulsion. I stayed in that position until the sickness passed then I wiped my mouth and sat up.

"Where's Koran?" I asked and looked back out to the water.

"He made it to the boat," Stephanie replied and I could hear the judgment in her voice.

"Did one of his keys work?"

She shrugged and pointed out into the sea. "He's on his way back."

I sulked and lowered my head. It was strange that at this age I could still feel embarrassment, but the shame of my failure burned to my core.

"Dad get up," Alistair called.

He reached out his hand and I took it. Grunting, I pulled myself up and balanced on wobbly legs. I gripped his shoulder for balance and blinked my eyes wildly.

"You okay?"

"Yeah...I'll be alright."

The wind died down and the water seemed much calmer than it had been when I was fighting for my life. Koran motored the sailboat toward the remaining piece of the pier and waved at us with a gleeful face that felt like a punch in the chest.

"Let's go," I grumbled.

Koran was able to pull the boat a few feet from the dock with ease. He ran along the side of the hull and tossed a rope out.

"Tie this to something. Make it tight!" he shouted.

I took the rope and looped it around one of the massive beams then we gathered all the bags and started to toss them to Koran. After that I helped David and Charlie onto the little trampoline webbing up front. Melinda and Stephanie went next, followed by Ashley and Alistair.

I boarded last and untied the line before I jumped in. I pulled the rope with me then leaned back to catch my breath. My head still felt groggy, but my pride hurt much more than that.

"Hey," Koran said as he grabbed my arm to help me steady. "Don't worry about earlier, that could've happened to anyone."

I hung my head in shame and snorted in agreement. Koran stared at me then gasped.

"That looks pretty bad. Stephanie found a medical kit in one of the other boats. You should let her stitch that up before we get moving."

I touched the side of my head and felt the warm blood as it trickled freely. "Yeah...yeah I guess."

Stephanie was all too eager to play doctor with my face. I had no idea how painful seven stitches could be without anesthetic. I felt every stab and tug of my skin like she was trying to peel my face off.

Once she finished she doused it with antiseptic and cold sea water that hurt just as bad as the stitches did. She said it should heal nicely and according to Koran she'd been a nurse in the Navy.

"So how do we get this thing moving?" I asked Koran and found myself a seat on the back deck.

"Well, the wind died down and I don't wanna try motoring all the way to the base. We might need the gas later. So for now, we wait."

It didn't seem like much of a plan and I didn't like the idea of being anywhere near the unstable marina, but what did I know. I didn't have a plan of my own and I'd already proven how inept I was at surviving on the sea. So, for the time being, Koran was our captain.

Melinda took the kids inside then raided the kitchen. All of the electronics worked on the boat including the stove, which was a serious benefit. She found the pantries were stocked with food and there was a deep freezer full of meat.

"I'm cooking...any requests?" she asked.

"Spaghetti!" David shouted.

No one objected so spaghetti it was. Melinda started cooking and I spent my time rummaging through the boat. I found flares, more clothes and a log that detailed the last trip the boat had been on.

I took a seat on a pillow and started to thumb through the pages. They'd sailed to Miami, Ft. Lauderdale, even took a trip down to the Bahamas once. It was a lifetime of memories committed in ink.

The log was pretty detailed. I surmised the owners name was Chuck and it seemed like he had a thing for parties with college girls. He even listed his various bedroom conquests and what he liked about each one of them.

Juxtaposed next to those entries were trips he'd taken with his wife and family. Some of them were only days apart. I guess nothing was ever as it seemed.

As I closed the book a picture fell out and I picked it up. There was a group of four men with sun burnt faces and shades on. They were holding a Mahi Mahi and grinning from ear to ear. I flipped the picture over.

"Had a blast in the Keys Chuck. We'll have to do it again."

The note was scribbled in the center. It was crazy to think that Chuck and whoever had written the note were probably dead now. Hell, for all I knew everyone in that photo was dead. Life was fickle like that, I guess it always had been, but now it was just right in my face.

The smell of fresh food ripped me from my thoughts. I set the book down and made my way to the kitchen where Stephanie was arranging plates. It was the first time in weeks we'd had real food, something that hadn't been freeze-dried and packaged away for years.

"I could get used to this," Koran said as he swallowed a mouthful of noodles.

"All we're missing is some lobster," I joked.

"I promise you Randall, no matter how hungry I get, any lobster you find is all yours," Melinda said with a smile.

"Remember you said that."

Alistair and Ashley sat away from everyone. They whispered to one another and shot suspicious glances in our general direction.

Koran huffed, "Those two need to join the group."

"Let em be," I retorted. "It's gotta be hard to be a teen in all of this. Stuck in between two worlds. It's good they can talk with each other."

"I guess so. The apocalypse can bring out the loner in anyone."

I shrugged. I didn't see it that way, but everyone had an opinion. Alistair had been away from his phone, his TV and his game for I didn't even know how long. Interaction with another human his age was a good thing as far as I was concerned.

After everyone had eaten their fill we cleaned up and lounged around in the saloon. Stephanie and Mclinda talked about kids and work among other things while David and Charlie explored the boat. Alistair and his new girlfriend sat in the corner making googly eyes at one another and I headed out onto the deck with Koran.

"It's getting dark," I said and looked up. "Can we sail in the dark?"

"We could, but not worth the risk. We'll motor closer to that island over there and drop anchor for the night." he pointed.

"Then what?"

"At day break we'll head to MacDill. What do you think you're going to find there anyway?"

I shrugged. "I don't know. You tell me, you worked there."

"I'm not saying it's not a good idea. But if they're gone...if you don't find any answers, then what?"

"I don't know. I mean, there has to be somebody somewhere. We can't be the only people left in the state...the world."

"I guess you're right. I don't know what to think anymore. We just survived a fucking earthquake."

We both laughed and I thought about Steve again. I wondered if he was still alive. I wondered if anyone I knew was still alive.

"Well let's get moving," Koran said, interrupting my thoughts. "Shouldn't take more than ten minutes to cross the channel and drop anchor over there. We can stick to the leeward side for the night, it should keep us in good shape in case that storm hits."

An hour later I realized Koran was full of shit. We were all huddled together in the saloon as the rain and wind battered the ship like a drunk husband. The sound of rain pellets thundering against the glass made Charlie shriek as flashes of lightning illuminated the bay.

I couldn't see the water outside, but I could feel it smashing against the hull. It was so violent I was convinced we were experiencing another earthquake.

"We're gonna be okay, right?" Melinda asked.

"Yeah, yeah we should be fine. Ships have to weather storms all the time. This thing is good to go."

I was lying. I had no clue and I'd already proven how ineffective I was in the water. If it came down to it, I'd be the first to drown. Although I could've sworn at one point in my life I was part fish.

My stomach churned and twisted as the boat swayed from left to right. I groaned and closed my eyes which only made it worse. I fought the urge to vomit and tried to will myself to feel better.

"I thought you said this was the good side of the island?" I shouted over the roar of wind.

"It is. Trust me, it's much worse on the other side."

I nodded, hiding the feeling that Koran didn't know what he was talking about. Another flash of lightning sizzled my eyeballs and a clap of thunder shook the windows. Charlie climbed onto me like a monkey and David tucked himself into a ball.

"This sucks," Alistair groaned.

He was right, but we were in it now and had no choice, but to ride it out. So with Charlie wrapped around me like a boa constrictor, I pushed back into a corner and sat down.

The storm raged on for the rest of the night like it had a vendetta against all mankind. The rain sounded like rocks being thrown and the howling wind and massive waves tried desperately to sink the boat.

In all of that, at some point I fell asleep. I was worn out as I'm sure everyone else was. Being at anchor during a storm wasn't the safest of places, but compared with everywhere else we'd had to sleep, this was a five-star hotel.

I awoke to the sounds of everyone else snoring, deep, grunting noises that only came from pure exhaustion. It was before dawn and the sun was still hiding behind the horizon. If it wasn't for my anxiety, I probably would've continued to sleep well into the afternoon.

Inside of the saloon it was nice and warm thanks to the heater and the extra parka I'd found. During the night, I'd laid Charlie down in his sleeping bag and he seemed to be in heaven. I couldn't complain either as it was the best sleep I'd had in weeks. I was really starting to appreciate the little things.

With a yawn and a stretch, I walked out onto the deck and stared out across the water. It looked calm and silvery, reflecting the bits of light that crept out from the sun's bed. Palm leaves and debris floated across the surface and every now and then a fish would splash then disappear.

The boat had done well. We'd either stowed everything away or strapped it down with bungee rope and I was pleased to see that it all had survived.

Shivering, I tightened my jacket and sucked in a lungful of the cool, moist air. The weather was calm now and the light wind that blew against my face was better than a gallon of coffee.

To my left there was a waterlogged box wrapped in red and black cord. I unstrapped it and decided to rift through the contents. Most of it was soggy clothes and plastic wrapped flairs. But down in the bottom I found a pair of binoculars.

I pulled them out then took a seat on the floor. The water gently lapped against the sides of the boat and I leaned my head back and listened to the soothing lullaby. The rhythmic splashing was hypnotizing and I found myself drifting away.

This was my first real chance to stop and think about everything that had gone on. At first I tried to make sense of what was happening and everything Koran had told me, but that was useless. Nothing made sense.

Instead, I thought about my old life. It felt like it was Tuesday. I really had no reason to think that, but something, maybe my body's internal calendar just screamed Tuesday. That meant basketball for David and....my mind paused. We had missed Christmas.

"Wow!" I said to myself.

The holiday had come and gone while we were traipsing around in the woods. It was crazy how meaningless things like that became. The kids hadn't even noticed it, I guess we were all a little too busy running for our lives.

I was pretty sure we were in late January. We'd missed the new year and everything. The kids would've been back in school by now, but I was sure their school no longer existed.

"Over there," I heard a voice on the wind.

I opened my eyes and shook my head. I was certain my mind was playing tricks on me and what I'd really heard was the caw from a seagull. But then I heard a clunking noise and a splash.

I jumped up and looked around the empty bay. We were the only boat on the water, at least the only one that hadn't sunk. I thought, maybe it was a dolphin or something playing around in the shallows.

"Hurry up," I heard the voice again.

It was distant and carrying across the water, but it was definitely someone talking. I looked toward the shore and only saw blurry objects through the lightening fog. Maybe something was moving over there, but it was hard to tell.

"The binoculars," I mumbled.

My fingers tightened around them and I pulled them to my eyes. Glaring through the magnified glass, I stared toward the shore. At first there was nothing but blurs of rock and sand. I adjusted the magnification and looked again.

"No!" I grimaced.

Turning on my heels, I rushed back inside of the saloon. "Wake up!" I shouted. "We have to go now!"

Melinda popped up with crazy eyes and glared at me in confusion. Koran jumped to his feet and spun around in a circle like he was trying to find something to hit.

"What is wrong with you?" he snapped at me.

"Everything okay?" Melinda asked in a groggy voice.

Before I could answer I heard the grumble of a motor. Whipping around, I ran back out to the deck and stared through the binoculars again.

A small red and white boat was bouncing across the water headed straight for us. Three very familiar men were on board, two of them were sitting in the front with shotguns already pointed in our direction.

My mind flashed back to a woman screaming for help. She was half naked and crawling across the road, crawling away from three men that were going to rape and kill her and now here they were heading for us. This was karma.

The black guy was steering the boat and the two brothers were leaning on the rails, trying to steady their aim. They had spotted us and they were on the way to do what they did best.

Something inside of me shouted no! I wouldn't let this happen. I couldn't help the woman earlier, but now I had to stop them.

"Koran!" I yelled. "How the hell do we start this thing?"

Koran followed me onto the deck and narrowed his eyes. "You know them?" he asked.

"Not exactly, but I know they don't want to discuss the weather over a glass of wine."

"We can't outrun them in this."

"Well shit, just give up now then," I said and threw my hands into the air. "We have to try something, get this shit moving!"

Koran looked at me for a moment like he didn't plan on doing anything. Maybe he was still half asleep or maybe he really didn't give a shit. But I knew what kind of men those were back there and I didn't plan on my wife becoming their next victim.

"Koran!" I shouted again with anger in my voice.

"St... start the engine. I'll get the anchor and get the sails ready," he replied.

"I don't know how," I retorted.

"Just turn the damn key and push the sticks forward. Jesus, have you ever been on a boat."

I wanted to punch Koran in the eye, but we didn't have time to argue. Besides, I probably needed to reserve my anger and energy for the rapist that were headed our way. Fuming, I ran back inside and headed for the cockpit.

"What's going on?" Melinda asked.

"People are coming this way, people with guns."

Melinda's face lit up with fear. She slid closer to Charlie and David, who were still sleeping and wrapped her arms around them.

"Oh my God!" Stephanie shrieked. "Where's Koran?"

"He's dealing with the sails."

I ran through the saloon and into the cockpit. To the right there was a captain's chair and a large silver wheel.

I jumped into the seat and twisted the key that dangled from the ignition. I heard the sound of the engines churn and then I pushed the two levers slightly forward. The boat jolted then slowly started to move.

"Thank God," I mumbled.

The bow rocked up and down, gliding over the small waves. I turned the wheel and we started to come around the island and I felt the wind push the boat from side to side.

"Is that them?" Stephanie asked.

I followed her finger out to the left and saw the motorboat zipping toward us. At the speed they were going, they'd be on top of us in a few minutes. They were probably close enough to shoot us already.

"Can you take the wheel?" I turned to Stephanie and asked. "I'm gonna check on Koran."

"Sure," she replied in a shaky voice.

I stepped around her and headed toward the deck. "Take the kids below," I said to Melinda. "Keep them down there until this is over."

"I can help," Alistair blurted out.

"No... just keep your head down."

"Dad this is a big boat, it's gonna take more than two of you to keep it safe. I can help."

"We're all gonna have to help," Stephanie said. "Ashley can go below deck with the kids."

Before I could reply Koran stumbled into the cockpit. His face was covered in sweat and he had scratches on his forearms. He glared around with an anxious look then took the wheel from Stephanie.

"We need to head for the base. With the sails up, we're still not gonna get enough speed," he said then turned to me. "We have to keep them from boarding."

"Randall," Melinda cringed.

"Keep us going straight," Koran said as he shifted over so Stephanie could take control again.

He grabbed his rifle and I followed his lead and took my pistol out of my bag. Melinda was staring at me with watery eyes and I could feel her worry.

"Randall," she said again.

I wished I had some words to put her at ease, but there were none. It seemed this life, this new world that we were living in was nothing more than crisis after crisis. Around every corner there was another pitfall waiting to take your life.

"Keep your head down," I told her and gave her a kiss then turned to Alistair. "Stay in here. If anything happens to me, you keep your mom and brothers safe."

He clenched his jaw and nodded. I pulled him close and gave him a hug. I knew he'd do whatever needed to be done. Over the last several weeks Alistair had become a new person, we all had. We were stronger now and that gave me hope that we might survive.

"Get us to the base," Koran told Stephanie. "I won't be able to adjust the sails so hopefully the wind will last." He glanced at me and tipped his head toward the rear deck. "Let's go."

169

I followed him outside with my gun clenched tightly. The wind had picked up and a salty mist was spraying into the air. I grabbed the rail to steady myself as the boat leaned to one side.

"Stay on the aft deck, I'm gonna head to the top," Koran shouted over the wind.

"Stay where?"

"Back here, don't let them get close or they'll probably shoot the engines."

I looked at the gun in my hand and then back over the water toward the speeding boat. Koran must've read my mind because he sighed and reached for the gun.

"Here you go," I said and handed it to him.

He looked at it for a moment. Then started pulling things and flipping levers like some magician. After a few moments, he handed me the gun back and grinned.

"Just point and shoot," he said. "You've got twelve bullets. Do you have any more magazines?"

"Any more what?"

"Bullets?"

"Oh, clips. Yeah, I have two more in my pocket."

"Ok, if you pull the trigger and nothing happens, press this button here and the magazine will fall out. Don't lose it. Put it in your pocket and put one of the new ones in then press this button," he pointed.

"I got," I replied.

"Good luck."

With that, Koran headed around the side of the boat toward the front. I walked down the steps toward the water and sat down. I stared at the trail of churning froth behind us and took a deep breath.

The guys on the boat hadn't seen me yet, but they were angling like they planned to broadside us. I could only imagine what they'd do if we let them get on. I just couldn't let that happen.

The whining engine grew louder and louder as it chopped through the water. I could hear the constant splashing of their boat jumping from wave to wave as they closed in behind us.

I took a deep breath, trying to ready myself for whatever was about to happen. Normally I'd be terrified and the threat of death would render me almost useless. But today felt different. I'd stared death in the face too many times, survived too much, and the more I thought about these assholes, the less I feared them.

This was a fight I had to win. There were no uncertainties or ambiguities about it. My family depended on me and I knew I wouldn't let them down.

Over the sound of our own engines two echoing claps thundered. I ducked my head then peeked over the railing. Two sharp snaps answered back and I knew Koran was returning fire.

"What was that?" Alistair asked and pushed the door to the saloon open.

"Stay down!" I shouted at him just before a hail of pellets showered the side of the boat.

He quickly slammed the door and dove back inside. I raised up and pointed my gun toward their boat. I squeezed the trigger and death exploded from the barrel.

The gun nearly leapt from my hand and I fell back to the steps just to catch it. Coiling my fingers, I squeezed the gun tighter. Another clap sounded and I heard a thud near the backside of the boat. Four more snaps rang out from our end in response.

"I'm out of bullets!" Koran yelled.

Jumping to my feet, I aimed again and fired several more shots. I had no clue where any of my bullets went, but they certainly didn't land on my target. Cursing, I took cover back behind the wall.

Koran came running down the side of the boat and dropped to the deck as another shotgun blast sounded. I looked down at him, expecting some kind of game plan, but he seemed to be all out of ideas.

I could hear their engine slowing down and I leaned over the side to get a better look. They were less than twenty yards away and closing quickly.

Koran shouted something to me, but I couldn't make it out. I stood back up and steadied myself on the swaying deck. With one eye closed, I aimed for the center of their boat and squeezed the trigger until there were no bullets left. The dry click of my pistol felt like someone had sucked all of the power out of me.

One of the men on the bow slumped over and groaned. He tumbled over the front rail and splashed into the water. The boat made a loud thump and climbed up the water, then a stream of crimson snaked through the wake behind them.

"Keep shooting," Koran screamed.

I pressed the button he told me and the magazine fell from the bottom of the gun. I tried to catch it, but our boat crested over another wave and it went spiraling into the air.

"Shit!" I grumbled.

I lunged forward just as the boat rose and the railing slammed into my chest. With a mangled grunt, I collapsed onto the side and my gun slipped from my hand. It splashed into the water and vanished beneath the waves.

"Was that the fucking gun?" Koran asked in a scathing voice.

I nodded then ran back for the saloon.

"Where are you going?"

"Flare gun!"

I swung the door open and darted inside. Melinda and Stephanie looked mortified. I grabbed my bag then looked up at them.

"We're gonna be fine. Just keep heading toward the base."

I grabbed the flare gun and paused. "Everything is okay," I said. "I promise."

Once I got back outside the motorboat had already pulled alongside us. Koran was wrestling with one of the twins as he tried to climb aboard. The other twin had his shotgun raised and was trying to get a clear shot.

Without breaking stride, I raised the flare gun and aimed. I pulled the trigger and the flare whistled from the barrel and hit the man with the gun square in the chest.

His face froze in shock and agony. His fingers loosened and the shotgun fell from his limp hands. Without a sound, he fell backwards and tumbled into the ocean.

"No!" the other twin yelled and swung his hands wildly.

I quickly descended the steps to help Koran. The man had his shirt and was pulling at him while punching him in the head with the other hand.

"Get off!" I shouted and threw a punch of my own.

It connected with a thud to the side of his head and he roared. Straining, I tried to pry his hands off of Koran. He twisted and grabbed me by the collar instead.

I lost my balance as our boat crashed into another wave then slammed into the side of his. The momentum carried me up and before I knew it, me and the burly twin plummeted over the side and into the freezing water.

CHAPTER 20

WE FIGHT AND THEN WE FIGHT SOME MORE

For the second time in less than two days I found myself fighting against an icy, cold death. I was convinced that the sea wanted nothing more, but to kill me and now they'd sent a stocky, murdering rapist to help.

I pulled myself to the surface and breathed like a newborn baby. I had a split second to look around before I felt the sting of the twin's fist smash into the back of my head. It was a jarring blow that almost rendered me unconscious. A glimpse of the sailboat motoring away was the last thing I saw.

I let out a whimper before my head plunged back under the water. The frothy slop spun me around and twisted me into knots. The cold black sea was winning and the rapist twin was doing his part to ensure a victory.

Darkness surrounded me, wrapped me up like a blanket and pulled me to its chest. Like an ominous lullaby the current swayed me back and forth. The slap of salty tears caressed my face as the lack of oxygen spurred delirium.

It was really amazing how the brain worked. Just when you think all is lost, it finds a way to push just a little more. The cold water was likely to freeze me to death before I drowned, but my mind had decided it wanted no part of that.

I was faintly aware that I was still in the ocean, but the only thing I could think of was the birth of Alistair. The memory was vivid, like I'd been transported back there to witness it all over again.

The smell of the hospital room flooded my nostrils even though I was submerged in the sea. It was so real, so lucid. I could feel the apprehension and fear of what we'd created. The excitement mixed with trepidation of the unknown.

We'd made a person. Somehow, through the wonders of nature the two of us had created our very own human. And it felt like I was right there, watching my first child take his first breath.

My heart thundered, beating enough for a million lifetimes. I felt complete. My life had finally been given purpose and there would be no greater accomplishment than being a father. It was the happiest day of my life, then it suddenly faded.

It was a shock to my system to watch the image vanish. I felt rage and anger that I couldn't see it, I couldn't pull it back. Then I realized something. That memory, that fleeting vision that sprung into my mind before I succumbed to the nebulous abyss was my brain fighting back. So, I let it.

"Kick you stupid bastard," a voice echoed inside of my head.

I snapped my legs once, then twice, then three times. I pulled at the water in desperation, the urge for oxygen fueling my arms. Over and over I crawled up, I pulled toward the air, toward life, toward my family.

I felt my head break the surface as the cold wind slammed into me. I gasped and swallowed the air in giant gulps. My lungs burned as they expanded and pushed out the gallons of salt water. I vomited into the sea then spun around to get my bearings.

The sun had broken through the clouds and the gray water glared like liquid silver. Not too far away, the red and white motor boat bobbed around in the jostling tide.

I wiped the water from my eyes and smiled at the sailboat that gleamed like a shinning beacon of hope. Koran had turned the boat around and was heading back for me. The wide catamaran smashed over the waves as it fought against the wind. I wasn't dead yet.

Neither was the man that tried to kill me. The surviving twin was swimming toward his own boat, but he hadn't gone far.

"Asshole," I grumbled.

With a deep breath, I kicked my legs and took off after him. Every stroke I took I felt more powerful. I was pulling the sea toward me, dragging him back into my grasp and this time I wouldn't lose.

He must've felt my presence, or heard me splashing in the water because he paused and turned around. His face lit up when he saw me and he started to paddle my way.

When he got within arms reached I lunged forward and grabbed his shirt. I swung my other hand into his face and smashed his nose with my palm.

His head lurched backwards and blood squirted into the water. He yelped then grabbed me around the neck and pulled me under.

Instead of fighting to get back to the surface, I decided to swim deeper. Wrapping my arms around him, I kicked hard and torpedoed toward the sea floor.

More saltwater funneled down my throat and I fought the urge to head back up. This had to be done. He was going to die, even if that meant I died with him.

I squeezed him tighter and flailed my legs like a frog. Like an anchor, we plunged into the unknown. The light faded and the water cooled as we sank deeper and deeper.

He tried to fight back, but it was useless, his fate had been sealed. The more he strained the more oxygen he burned, which only made my job easier. With my hands locked around him, we plummeted into the shadows.

My ears popped and my legs cramped from the cold. Clenching in pain, I kicked again and blew out the last bit of air in my lungs. Like a lead weight, I careened into the blackness, headfirst into a watery grave.

The twin gulped the ocean like a dying fish and his resistance started to fade. He gasped one last time then stopped moving. His body fell limp so I relaxed my arms and let him go.

He was suspended for a moment in the water. His pale skin almost glowing in the murky depths. With blank eyes, he started to float away, slowly drifting to his final resting place. Better than he deserved.

I watched him for a moment. Sailing further into the deep blue until I could no longer see him. He would never hurt anyone else.

With my last bit of strength, I turned and swam for the surface. The only thing that kept me going was the promise of life that existed on the other side. Every meter I moved was another tomorrow that I might be able to see.

The water warmed just a bit and I could feel life within my grasp. It urged me to kick harder, to fight more than I'd ever fought before. That's all life was now, fighting and then fighting some more.

I burst out of the water and inhaled a lungful of air. Leaning my head back, I huffed until my mind stopped spinning.

"Over here," Koran yelled.

I shifted until I could see the boat chopping against the waves. Koran threw out a life preserver and I clung to it like a leech. I laid my head against my arm and held tightly as he pulled me toward the boat.

"You're alive," he said in shock and held out his arm.

"Looks that way," I replied. Reaching forward, I grabbed his hand and pulled myself onto the back deck. I flopped to the floor and stared up to the sky in relief. For a brief moment, I relaxed, for a brief moment I was safe.

"Is everyone okay?" I asked instinctively.

"We're all good," Melinda said as she fell next to me and wrapped her arms around my shoulders.

I leaned my head into her and took a deep breath. I was alive, we all were and that brought me more joy than I'd felt in my whole life. It was the little things.

I could feel the boat start moving again and I slowly sat up. The engines groaned as we headed through the choppy waves. The bright yellow sails flapped about uselessly, riddled with holes from the shotgun pellets.

"You saved my life man," Koran said and poked his head out of the saloon. "I thought I was a goner."

I smiled at him and shrugged. "Don't mention it. I figured I owed you anyway."

"If you're feeling alright, you should come take a look," he said and held out the binoculars.

"What is it?"

"The base...you'll want to see this."

CHAPTER 21

SKELETON CREW

The boat rocked gently back and forth. Water gurgled underneath the bow with a low rumble that sounded like a drowning dog. The glow from the moon glistened over the water and I rubbed my hands together to keep warm.

"Anything? Koran asked.

He walked out of the saloon with two cups of coffee and handed me one. Steam floated from the surface and faded into the night.

"Thanks," I said.

"I don't know if coffee has an expiration date, but I figured it was something."

I nodded. "I haven't seen a single soul."

Koran took a seat next to me and groaned. I'd been out there for hours on the back deck, staring at the base. The boat bobbed back and forth at anchor, a reflection of our current situation as we mulled over what our next move would be.

I'd chosen the base because I thought we'd find answers. I thought we'd find the civilization that seemed to have vanished. But what we found was nothing close to that.

The base looked deserted. Every tower, every guard station we could see was empty. The wooden dock that lead up to the park was splintered and broken. Evidence of earthquakes and storms were everywhere, but amidst the destruction there were no people.

Sighing, I stared through the binoculars and scratched my head. All around the edge of the sea wall there were abandoned military vehicles. Humvees, large, cargo trucks, even a few APC's.

They were parked there with the doors wide open. Like everyone had just run away or something. It was a strange sight.

"So what do you think?" I asked Koran. He was the military expert so I was gonna defer to him.

"What choice do we have? We watched this shit for two days, we might as well head ashore."

"Let's go then," I replied.

That was it, we were heading back into the unknown. Aside from our skirmish a few days ago, I felt pretty safe at sea. We hadn't seen another person and I'd accepted that it was a good thing, but being back on land scared me.

It was more than the earthquakes and fires. It was more than the storms and deadly weather. It was people, they were our biggest threat now. I still didn't trust Koran and he'd saved my life. Who knew what we'd find back in the city?

We motored toward the base under the moonlight in silence. There was only the sound of the water against our bow. The soft whoosh was an eerie soundtrack to a deadly adventure.

"What's the plan when we get there?" Koran asked.

"I honestly thought this would've all taken care of itself. You know, I expected people here or...or something. I guess at this point we just take a look around and see what we see."

"And if we don't see anything?"

"We have to find someone, we have to find out what's going on."

I looked away from him and stared down at the water. How much of that did I believe? How much longer could I go on being the optimistic when everything I saw told me we'd never be safe again?

We slowed down as we approached the wooden deck. Pieces of it looked stable enough to stand on so we headed toward the largest block and pulled alongside it. Quietly, I hopped out and tied a line to one of the few remaining cleats.

"So are we all going ashore or what?" Koran asked as he scanned the darkness.

"I think we should check it out first, just the two of us."

"You should bring your boy."

"Why?"

"The commissary isn't far from here. There's a good chance they still have food and supplies. The more we can carry the better."

I considered it for a moment. The base was a ghost town and Alistair had proven himself. If it'd make our trip easier it didn't seem like a bad idea.

"Fine," I replied.

"You see anything?" Melinda asked as she crept up behind me and wrapped her arms around my waist.

"Nope, I thought you were still sleeping."

"Couldn't...too much going on."

I nodded. "We're gonna head ashore and take Alistair."

"For what?"

"To look for answers, or worst case find more food. We may be on our own for a lot longer."

I bent down and reached into a small box I'd found in the cockpit. There was a tiny, silver revolver inside and I handed it to Melinda.

"Keep this just in case. We shouldn't be gone long, but if anything happens," I pulled the flare gun from my waistband and handed that to her as well. "Shoot of one of these and we'll come running."

"This is probably a better idea," she said and held up the two yellow and black radios we'd found earlier. "How about I just call you?"

I turned the knob on mine and it crackled to life. "Testing, testing," I said.

"They work!"

"Well, keep the flare gun just in case we get out of range."

Melinda nodded. "Be safe out there."

"Of course. Where's Alistair?"

"He's sleeping."

I laughed and headed into the saloon. "He's gonna love this."

After waking Alistair up and situating the boat, we climbed onto the dock in silence. I pulled my bag over my shoulders then looked back to Melinda.

"We'll be quick," I said. "I promise."

She'll smiled then turned around as Ashley walked up behind her. She didn't say anything, she just stared at Alistair with puppy dog eyes. He stared back at her then turned to me.

"Is it okay if I hang back? It's probably good if they have a man here," he asked.

I laughed. "You're hardly a man Alistair."

"No... we need you with us," Koran jumped in. "We are really gonna need the extra hands."

Ashley frowned and Alistair sulked his shoulders. I gave Koran a confused look then grabbed Alistair's bag.

"I'll just carry both bags. Go ahead and stay, make sure you hold down the fort while we're gone."

Koran groaned and started walking down the pier.

"You sure dad?"

"Yeah, we'll be fine. Besides, I'd rather have you safe on the boat."

Alistair grinned then joined Ashley. They climbed to the front of the boat and sat down on the trampoline. Melinda smiled and I shrugged my shoulders and grinned.

"Well...I'm off."

With that I followed after Koran, down the pier and into the great unknown. He'd just made it to the sidewalk and was waiting while he pouted like he'd lost a game of scrabble. I didn't know what was up his ass, but I'd already concluded that I didn't care.

"Where to?" I asked Koran as I got closer.

He slowly turned to look at me then cocked his head to the side. "Your boy could really help us out there."

"He's just a boy. It's better he stays back."

"He's not a boy anymore. Look around Randall, things have changed."

"Well, I'll let him be a boy for a little longer. Now, which way do we go?"

"The main road is this way," he pointed and let out a frustrated sigh. "We should be able to see a good part of the base on the way to the commissary."

"Lead the way."

Koran turned and headed down the road. It was four o'clock in the morning and fog had blown in, covering the ground like a graveyard. It was spooky how deserted everything was. Every now and then a bird or some other creature would make a noise and I'd feel my heart stop, but we never saw another living person.

"What the hell happened to everyone?" I grumbled. "It's like, it's like they all vanished."

"Evacuated," Koran corrected me. "After they got the word out, it looks like they headed for the hills as well. I would've thought they'd staffed the command center here, but...doesn't look that way."

"This is bigger than flood warnings. Something else is going on."

"Maybe, maybe not. What the hell else could it be?

"That's the question isn't it."

I shrugged and continued down the two-lane street. Our pace was quick, but careful, every shadow or side street posed a threat that we had to be ready for. Things tended to go from calm to holy shit in no time.

A few of the street lights were still working and gave the fog an orange haze. It floated over the ground like some kind of toxic gas, reaching out to snag an unsuspecting life. I knew it was harmless, but I couldn't help but think it explained all the crazy shit I'd seen the last few months.

Knocked over trashcans rolled across the road as raccoons tumbled out of them, scavenging for anything they could find. The little family of three looked just as confused as we were, like they were suddenly cast into a world that no longer made sense.

"The commissary is that way," Koran pointed. But there's an administration building we can check out first."

"Sure, let's just be quick. I don't like being out here."

"Me neither, but we should check out the hangars too. We might be able to find something in there."

I nodded and continued walking. The sooner we got back to the boat, the better I would feel. Everything about the base seemed wrong. It was a bad idea to head to come here and deep down I hoped my decision wouldn't cost any lives.

We passed a long, green building and I paused. One of the lights inside was on and the glowing window stood out in the dark like a lighthouse. I called out to Koran when a sudden loud, crackle nearly made me piss myself and I jumped.

"Randall," Melinda's voice called.

I fumbled in my pocket and pulled out the radio. My heart was thumping against my chest with anxiety.

"Hello? What's wrong?" I gasped.

"Nothing," she quickly replied. "I just wanted to make sure everything was going okay."

"We're good. I said the radio was for emergencies only. You scared the hell out of me."

"Sorry, I was just checking on you. I'll go back to playing solitaire," Melinda replied then giggled.

"Don't worry about it. We'll be back soon."

I shoved the radio into my coat pocket and laughed to myself. Koran glanced at me and I shrugged and threw my hands into the air.

"Women," I said. "You want to check that out? The lights on."

Koran nodded and we made our way toward the rectangular structure. To my surprise the door wasn't locked and we walked right in.

There was a desk to my left with blank sheets of paper spread across it. The chair behind it was knocked over and a little golden lamp burned on the corner next to a cup of pens.

The front part of the building was a small office with sparse furnishings. Beyond that, there was a narrow hall that led toward the back and disappeared in the shadows.

"This way," I whispered.

We quietly tip-toed through the office and made our way down the hall. There were four rooms in the back, but each one was completely empty.

"What the hell is this place?"

"Some kind of administration office," Koran replied. "Let's just get to the commissary. There's nothing here."

He was right. There was no one here, I doubted anyone had been on the entire base for weeks. The whole trip was a mistake.

We headed back outside and walked down the street to the commissary. The electronic doors at the front were shattered and a few overturned carts were blocking the entrance.

"You watch much news Randall?" Koran asked as we slid the carts out of the way.

"A little."

"Yeah? There's always these stories of global warming...climate change. What do you make of any of that?"

"I don't know. Never given it much thought."

I stepped into the commissary and started looking around. I took a flashlight from my bag and swept it in wide beams in front of me. The shelves were nearly empty, but I grabbed the few items that were there and started tucking it into my bag.

"Looks like somebody's been here," Koran said as he picked up a dusty can. "They damn near cleaned the place out."

"Yeah...I really thought we'd find more."

"We can head out of the gate. There's some smaller stores tucked behind the apartments that might not have been hit."

I shrugged. "Let's just hurry up. We've been away long enough."

We left the commissary and headed out of the main gate. As soon as we walked off of the base it was like we entered a nightmare.

The whole city was on fire. Every building was ablaze, cars and debris smoldered like hot coals, sending dark, black smoke into the air. The asphalt was riddled with cracks and ugly fissures. Steam bellowed from the ground in long, dark spirals. I thought I'd seen destruction, but now...we were looking at the end of the world.

CHAPTER 22

CITY OF ASHES

"It's too dangerous. Let's just go back, it's not worth the risk," I said.

We were standing right outside of the gate, looking at the crumbling city. Koran wanted to go look around, but the multiple trenches and sea of fire was screaming something totally different.

"Look, I don't want to go out there either, but we have to."

I laughed. "We have to? We have to? Why the hell would we have to go out there?"

"This is the world now Randall," he replied and waved his hand toward the city. "Take a good look. There's nowhere left to run and no one to turn to. How long do you think we'll survive on that boat with the food and water we have? We need supplies, we need medicine, we need to be self sufficient. From now on, this is what we risk our lives for."

Koran had a point, although I didn't like it. We were already running low on supplies and I was sure things were gonna get worse. I needed to start thinking long term, even though the idea of that scared the hell out of me.

"Fine," I replied. "I'm not going far though."

Koran patted me on the shoulder and grinned. Still smiling, he headed down the warped sidewalk and into the burning city.

The thick, black smoke ruined our visibility. We walked side by side, struggling to avoid cracks and holes in the pavement. Fires raged all around us and I could feel the heat, threatening to singe the hairs on my arms.

"There's a convenience store a block down. We should check that out first," Koran suggested.

"If it's not on fire."

"You gotta be more optimistic man. "

"Fine, it's probably not on fire."

Koran laughed then sped up. I followed him slowly, the smoke was making my lungs burn and every few yards I stopped and fought off a coughing fit.

I felt like I was in a nightmare. Everything was crumbling to dust, falling apart and being swallowed by the tormenting flames. It was like a warzone in some third world country, but it wasn't. It was my home, it was America and I knew that it would never be the same.

We weaved in between a few apartment buildings that had managed to avoid being burned. After hopping over a fence, we squeezed through a row of hedges and ended up on the sidewalk right in front of the store.

It was mostly untouched by the fire. The smoke had stained the outside walls with soot, but beyond that, the store was fine. So, with a tiny bit of optimism, we headed inside and started looking around.

"See, no fire," Koran said happily. "Let's split up and grab what we can."

I cut my eyes and started scanning the aisles for anything we could take. The shelves were mostly empty or stocked with things like cat food and bleach.

I pulled a flashlight from my bag and headed further toward the back. A row of freezers with glass doors lined the far wall, but they were just as empty as everything else. After searching for ten minutes all I was able to find were a few bottles of water and some crackers that had expired a week earlier.

"How'd you make out?" I asked as I met Koran back near the front.

"Found some sodas and a few boxes of cereal. How about you?"

"The same more or less."

Koran sighed. "We're gonna need to head further. Maybe to one of the grocery stores or something. There's a target about a mile down."

I grunted, but it was swallowed by a loud explosion right outside. Koran snapped his head around and jumped into me. A blazing orange light flared and illuminated the store front. The fire had made it to us.

"We gotta go!" I yelled.

Without another word, we rushed outside. The fire was only a few yards from the store and sweeping quickly in our direction. Another fissure opened up in the ground and was spewing flames into the air like a dragon. Everything it touched erupted in a brilliant orange and melted into nothing. The city was imploding.

"This way!" Koran screamed and rushed around the back of the store.

I followed behind him as we weaved between burning cars and patches of scorched lawn. It seemed like every time we made some headway, we were forced backwards by a wall of fire.

The apartments behind us started to crumble as the fire worked its way through the support beams. With a thundering crash, the roof caved in and splinters of wood and debris shot out like bomb fragments.

"Watch out!" I yelled and tackled Koran to the ground.

The shower of building fodder sailed over our heads and pinged off of the burning cars. In shock, we clamored to our feet, checked ourselves for any wounds then kept running.

More fires erupted as ashes drifted into the air, igniting everything they touched. The thick smoke continued to make it hard to breath and even harder to see. Every street we turned down was a raging inferno with black plumes reaching out like the fingers of death.

"How the hell are we gonna get out of here?" I screamed as panic started to set in.

"This way!" Koran suddenly shouted.

He sprinted ahead and for a minute I thought his plan was to run directly into the fire. But as we got closer I saw the line of cars that snaked through the inferno like a tunnel. They were lined up side by side in an abandoned car lot and the cars in the center hadn't been touched by the fire yet.

"Hurry up!" Koran shouted.

He slid to a stop beside the first car and smashed the window with his elbow. Reaching in, he unlocked the door and dove inside then slid out of the opposite door. Without looking back, he headed to the next car and did the same.

I followed behind him and earned a few shards of glass in my leg for my carelessness. But I'd rather pay that price than burn to death.

We went from car to car across the lot as the fire burned closer and closer on both ends. Some cars we just climbed on top, but many were conversion vans or tall SUV's that would've been more trouble than it was worth. As luck would have it about half of them were opened and we managed to avoid any broken glass at all.

I could see the end getting close, but I could also feel the heat from the fire like I'd shoved my face into an oven. It was gonna be close and I could only pray that we would reach the end before the fire reached us.

"Move your ass!" I yelled to Koran as I sped up.

The increasing heat had me frantic. I dove through the backseat of the next car and nearly ran Koran over. This may have been his idea, but if Koran didn't get the hell out of my way I was going to go through him.

The metal popped and pinged on the cars on either side of us as the fire neared them. The frames started to warp and the paint melted like slices of cheese. I could hardly see through the thickening smog even though the sun was slowly starting to rise.

We rushed through the lot and as we reached the last car, I felt like we might survive. Koran bashed in the window and we quickly slipped through and came out of the other side.

Sighing, I stopped and took a quick glance behind us. Everything was either ashes or burning to the ground. Flames were still shooting out from the pavement like the earth had become a giant barbecue grill.

"Come on," Koran said and ran back toward the gate.

We slowed down once we made it to the commissary. The fires were far behind us and the base seemed safe, at least for now.

"We're gonna need gas," Koran said as we walked through the vacant streets. "I don't wanna risk being on the boat without it and the trip here cost us a lot."

"I guess," I replied sharply.

It sounded to me like he was blaming me for the base being deserted, but he didn't have a better idea. Koran was really starting to push my buttons and every time something didn't go right, he had a comment. I guess he forgot this was my show and he didn't have to be here.

"Can't believe we didn't find anything. I was really hoping the base would be worth it," Koran continued.

"You got any better ideas?" I asked defensively.

"Any place would be better than here right now," Koran chuckled.

I clenched my jaw, holding back the words I really wanted to tell him. I'd figured in my head that as soon as I was comfortable sailing the boat, Koran and his weird ass family had to go.

"If I could find a helicopter, I'd get the hell out of here," Koran continued. "Could really get a look at what's going on from up there."

"Yeah...maybe."

"We're gonna need something more than that sailboat eventually. We need to cover more ground."

"Water," I replied.

"Yeah whatever it is...we need to cover more of it."

"Well it is what it is, we make the best with what we have right now."

"The boat!" Koran shouted.

"Yeah, we have the boat. That's what I'm saying."

"No," Koran said then grabbed my shoulder and nudged toward the peer. "Where the hell is the boat?"

CHAPTER 23

COMING INTO THE LIGHT

The morning sun glowed with a fierce glare. The reflection was like an explosion of diamonds, burning in the sky, casting a brilliant light across the glittering water. It was beautiful, but it was empty.

We'd left the sailboat tied up to the dock and now there was nothing. The boat was gone, the lines were gone and any trace of our family was gone.

"What the fuck!" Koran shouted as he spun in place.

I stared out over the water in silence. I knew the boat had to be somewhere out there and I just needed to find them. I wished I'd brought the binoculars with me, but wishing wasn't gonna help now.

"Where the fuck are they? What the fuck!" Koran continued to yell.

"Calm down," I replied.

"Calm down? Calm down! Your family is missing, my family is missing. How the hell can you say calm down."

"Because you idiot. Did it ever occur to you that maybe they had to leave? Maybe someone was on this base and you're screaming like a fucking moron."

Koran gasped and then looked back toward the base with wide eyes. He seemed to get the picture and had decided to keep his mouth shut. Sighing, I stuffed my hands into my jacket pocket and racked my brain for an idea.

My hand hit something hard and I nearly screamed with excitement. I gripped the radio and yanked it out.

"Koran," I called and held up the little black and yellow device.

His face reflected mine as his lips morphed into a full on smile. I took a deep breath then pressed the transmit button.

"Melinda? Melinda are you there?" I called.

The wait was torture. The silence felt like someone was squeezing my head. Every second that passed that she didn't respond, was a lifetime of dancing barefoot across a floor of needles.

"Melinda?" I said again.

A bolt of static crackled from the other end and I jumped. Koran tried to grab the radio out of my hand and I shoved him back.

"I just want to hear it," he said.

I held the radio between the two of us. It crackled again and then a garbled voice seeped through. We both held our breath in anticipation, but the radio fell silent again.

"Melinda!" I shouted.

"Dad," Alistair's voice replied in a whisper. "Dad, we're in trouble."

"Alistair where are you?"

"I don't know some guys found us. They...they took mom, Stephanie and Ashley somewhere. Dad come quick."

I could feel my heart beating in my throat. So much adrenaline rushed through my body I couldn't stand still. My chest heaved up and down and I felt like I was going to pass out.

"Alistair, what do you see? What's around you?"

"We're on some island dad. Wait, there coming back."

"Jesus," I mumbled.

The radio was shaking so violently it was hard for me to hold it. Koran grabbed my hand and steadied it as we both waited. I could feel his anxiety and he only masked it by grinding his teeth together.

"You little shit!" I heard a voice snap from the radio. "Who the hell were you talking to?"

"No... please just let us go," Alistair shouted.

Then I heard him scream and the radio went dead.

"Alistair! Alistair!" I yelled over and over. "We have to find them," I huffed and turned to Koran. "We have to find them now."

"I know, I know," he replied.

I ran back to the edge of the dock and looked back over the water. "He said they were on an island."

"There's no island around here Randall," Koran replied grimly.

"They can't be that far...they just can't be."

Koran scratched his head and looked back into the bay. "Beer Can Island!" he suddenly shouted. "That's it!"

"How the hell do we get there?"

"There's gotta be something that floats on this fucking base," Koran snapped. "Let's go."

He wheeled around and started back down the street. I lingered for a moment then followed after him.

"There's a boat yard down here. They used to store canoes," Koran said.

We headed toward a chain-link fence behind a small garage. Boats on trailers were spread out across the ground, most were rusted and broken. But toward the back I could see a short row of green canoes.

We reached the fence and I yanked at the heavy chain that held it closed. "How the hell do we get in here?"

Koran jumped on the fence and started climbing. "Like this," he said.

Before I could reply the sound of a bullet hitting metal rang out. I dropped to the floor as Koran fell from the fence and covered his head. Another bullet hit the dirt next to me and I knew it was time to run.

Jumping to my feet, I took off in the direction we'd come. I didn't know where the shooting was coming from and I didn't care. I knew that where I was standing, wasn't safe.

"Come on!" I yelled to Koran, who was dragging ass.

Without slowing down, I rammed my shoulder into the rickety, wooden door of the garage and sped inside. Koran came tumbling after me.

The place stunk like a locker room for players that refused to bathe. It was empty except for a pile of random debris that had been swept into the center. There was a small, window on the side wall and another door at the rear of the garage.

"Get up," I said to Koran while I peeked out of the window.

There was a group of five men in fatigues, slowly working their way toward us. They'd been hiding behind the administration buildings on the next street. I could tell from the way they moved, that they were trained and they meant business.

"It's the fucking military," I groaned. "Why the fuck would the military be shooting at us."

Koran wrinkled his face and stared down at the ground. "They could think we're anybody. No matter how you shake it up we're trespassing on a military base."

His answer sounded legit, but I saw the look in his eyes. Koran was hiding something and if we lived through this I was going to find out what the hell it was.

"We gotta get out of here, they're coming to the door," I said and moved toward the back.

I twisted the handle on the rear door and gave it a gentle nudge. It opened slightly and I took a quick glance outside. If we hurried there was a straight shot to the commissary between a row of smaller offices. We could hide in there, or at least have time to come up with a real plan.

"We can make it to the commissary," I said. "Let's go."

I shoved the door the rest of the way open and took off. I didn't look to see if Koran was behind me, but from the sound of the huffing, someone certainly was.

I ran as fast as my legs would move through the narrow corridor created from the buildings. My head was tuckered low, fearing at any minute the soldiers would be behind us and firing at will. But they weren't and we made it inside safely.

"What the hell was that about?" I asked and kneeled behind one of the empty shelves.

"I don't know man, but we can't stay in here."

I looked at him sideways and tried to catch my breath. Koran was getting shadier by the minute and I was having a hard time trusting him.

"You hear me?" he asked.

"Yeah...can't stay here. What's the plan?"

Koran looked around and started heading down the far aisle. He waved his hand and begrudgingly I followed.

"Where the hell are we going?"

"The stock room is in the back. Hopefully we can get out of the loading docks before they figure out where we are."

His sentence was punctuated with the sound of automatic gunfire. Bullets tore through the empty shelves and exploded into the drywall. I fell to the floor and scurried after Koran, but a hail of lead slammed into the ground in front of me and cut me off.

Koran took a glance back then sped off into the stock room. I scowled at him then slid behind a shelf. I could hear the sound of the soldier's boots across the dirty tile. They were getting close and I didn't have anywhere to go.

"Shit," I grumbled under my breath.

I peered around the far side and it looked clear. As quietly as I could, I got to my feet and started to duck walk toward the next set of shelves. If I could just repeat that six times, I'd be outside and might have a chance.

Getting to the first three shelves was easy, but as I looked toward the fourth I could hear someone's steps closing in on me. I froze and tried to make out which direction they were coming from. The commissary had become eerily silent and my heart was thundering in my ears. Each beat sounded like a war drum, each step like the invading army.

With a deep breath, I pushed on. I was nearly to the next shelf when I heard a raspy voice shouting commands.

"Freeze! Don't move another muscle!" the man said.

I stopped dead in my tracks and swallowed. Clenching my jaw, I thought of Melinda and the kids and damned myself for ending up here. I should've been trying to save them, but I couldn't save myself.

"Don't shoot," I said and slowly turned around.

The man jolted his gun at me, but didn't fire. His sand colored fatigues were stained with blood and I wondered if it was his. He had a good amount of stubble covering his angled jaw and his eyes beamed like a stop sign.

"Who the hell are you?" the man shouted. "What are you doing here?"

Before I could answer another soldier stopped beside him and gave me a quick once over.

"It's not him Decker, let's go."

Both of the men turned around and immediately headed back toward the stock room. It took a moment for the shock to wear off of me. Then I collected myself and ran as fast as I could outside. I darted across the street and stopped in the parking lot of an office building.

Dark clouds had swept in and the sun was stuck behind them. A moderate wind was pushing around the palm trees and it seemed to be gaining strength. Another storm was brewing and I didn't want to be here when it hit. I needed to get to the island and I needed to find my family and I didn't know how the hell to even start.

As I stood there, trying to devise a plan another soldier rushed out of the commissary. He whipped his head back and forth like he was searching for something then paused as he spotted me.

I stared back at him, unsure of what to do. He looked just as confused as I was, like he wanted to wave, but then he suddenly raised his rifle and sent a triplet of shots toward me.

I dove to the ground in panic then scurried around the side of the building and ran for my life. Bullets whizzed by my head and cracked into the pavement beside my feet.

Skidding like a race car, I turned down a side street and picked up my pace. The rumble of thunder droned across the sky like cannons and I couldn't hear if the soldier was still shooting or not. I turned around another corner then made a hard left between a row of portables. Huffing, I slowed to a jog.

As I passed the portables a long green barrack came into view. I made a beeline for it and increased my speed.

"Randall," a voice called from behind me.

I turned around and saw no one. The thunder rumbled a little louder and I felt a chill run up my back.

"Over here," the voice said.

I turned to the side and saw Koran waving from one of the portables. I quickly made my way toward him and he ushered me inside and closed the door.

"Shit man, I didn't think you were gonna get out of there," he huffed.

"You left me you asshole."

"Oh, come on man. What was I supposed to do? I had no guns and there were five of those guys. I found you didn't I?"

I took a deep breath and sat down on the floor. The portable was covered with a ratty, brown carpet and smelled like old cheese. A few broken chairs were tucked in the corner and discolored, yellow blinds covered the windows.

"We've gotta get to that island," I said as the thought of Melinda and the kids came rushing back to mind.

I stood up and cracked one of the blinds. There was no one outside and the sky was getting darker every second that passed.

"We can get out through the back door. Make it to the canoes before they see us," I suggested.

"We don't know where the hell they are and why the hell they're trying to kill us," Koran snapped.

"You," I replied.

"What?"

"They're trying to kill you."

"What the hell are you talking about?"

"You tell me Koran. Those guys in the commissary just let me go. They said I was the wrong guy, they were looking for you."

Koran dropped his eyes and turned away from me. He sighed then walked to the far wall and leaned against it.

"What are you not telling me?"

He didn't reply. He stared at the floor and tucked his hands into his pocket.

"Koran!" I snapped.

"I don't know who the hell these people are. That's the truth. Maybe I know why they are shooting at us."

"Well..."

"It... it's nothing really. Maybe I stole something from the base."

"Stole what?"

"Supplies. Guns, grenades, you know things I thought I'd need. So I guess when they saw me it was open season."

"So where is any of this shit now?"

"I told you about what happened in my neighborhood. Everything I had, got used then. Look it's not a big deal. We just need to get to the boats and get to the island. Once we're off the base we have nothing to worry about."

"So these people are trying to kill you because you stole some fucking guns?"

Koran groaned and straightened up. "You want to debate this or do you want to go get your kids?"

I bit my lip and swallowed. "We aren't done with this," I said and jabbed my finger at him.

"Okay, okay."

With that, I pushed myself to my feet. "Let's go," I grumbled and headed to the back of the portable.

I reached for the door, but it suddenly swung open and flew off of the hinges. It hit me in the chest and I fell back and landed on the floor under it.

Grunting, I pushed the thin metal to the side. My head was pounding and I'd split my lip down the middle. I covered my face and winced then gasped in shock.

The soldiers stormed into the room and circled us. They had their guns aimed and looked ready to kill us both.

I slowly found my feet and stood up then looked to Koran. He was staring at one of the men with a disdainful look. The man stepped forward and lowered his rifle. He glared at Koran then shook his head from side to side and grinned.

"Colonel Meyers," he said in an odd tone.

Koran glared back at him and puffed up his chest. "Major Clark."

CHAPTER 24

WHAT IS THE MAYFLOWER

"I'm glad to see you and the boys are doing well. Even though you're missing a few. Decker, Lockship, Hunter, Shipley...you look good," Koran said as if he was talking to old friends.

I scratched my head and scoffed. It felt like I was in the twilight zone. These guys had been trying to kill us for the last hour and now they were best friends.

"Can't say we're as happy to see you Colonel," Major Clark replied.

"Wait...wait!" I blurted. "You know them?"

Koran shrugged and twisted his face.

"What the hell is going on?" I continued.

Clark started to laugh. "Koran used to be our brigade commander. That's until he went AWOL and kidnapped the President's daughter."

"What!?"

"I don't have time to explain. Look she's in trouble and you guys can help," Koran righteously spoke.

"Why the hell would we help you? Tell us where she is and maybe we don't shoot you right now."

"You help me and I'll get you in Mayflower," Koran replied as if he'd offered them a million dollars.

All five of the soldiers started laughing. They shared skeptical glances with one another and looked at Koran like he'd lost his mind.

"It's not real," Clark spat, still chucking.

"It is and that girl is our ticket. You can come with me, you all can. Just help me get her back."

"We'll get her back alright, but not for you. Did you forget who the hell you work for?"

"The president is dead!"

"The first lady isn't. There's still structure, we still report to someone."

"And that someone will give us anything we want for bringing that girl back. That someone knows all about Mayflower."

"You stole her, so you could ransom her for access to a place that's not real? You've lost your shit Colonel. Mayflower is an urban myth."

"I saved that girls life. I just want what's mine in return."

"The secretary doesn't see it that way. He gave orders. You're as good as dead."

"Look Clark, you know me, you've known me for years. Mayflower is real...you know it. How much time do we have?"

I watched their exchange in shock. My bottom jaw was dragging across the filthy carpet and my brain was exploding.

"What?" Clark asked.

"You know as well as I do what's going on here. They tried to get everyone out and hell they did a good job with this county, but I'm sure they're cutting their loses. You guys ain't staying around. So how long?"

Clark looked around the room for a moment. He stared back at his men then sighed and looked back to Koran. "The helo leaves in an hour," he said reluctantly.

"Well fuck, help me Clark! Some assholes have that girl so whether you believe me about Mayflower or not we've gotta get her."

"And my family," I added in a shaky voice.

"Who the hell is this guy?" Clark asked as if he'd just seen me.

"This is Randall, they have his family too. So what do you say? Help us save them and I'll come quietly. Just give us a seat on the flight out of here."

"Out of here?" I echoed. "I'm not going anywhere with these guys."

Clark ignored me and turned back to Koran. "Fine, I'll play along. If the President's daughter is really there, I'll save her. If not, we're gonna bury you and your buddy. Lockship, Hunter and Shipley, head back and finish getting everything ready. We'll be along in a few."

"Yes sir," three of the men said and rushed outside without another word.

Decker was still standing next to Clark. He was glaring at Koran like he wanted to punch him in the face and I wished that he would.

He was a big guy, probably six foot six and well over two hundred pounds. He had dark spiky hair and a vein that bulged down the middle of his forehead like a power cable.

"You," Clark said and turned to me. "You can stay if you want, you and your family. Just know in 24 hours the entire state is gonna take a nose dive into the Atlantic."

My mouth fell open again and I turned to Koran. He gave me an odd look then stared at the ground.

"Alright," Clark boomed. "Where are these lost sheep?"

CHAPTER 25

THE RESCUE

Partnering with Clark and Decker was much better than the plan we had. For starters, they had a boat with an actual motor, and they had guns, lots of guns. But refused to give us any, apparently, I wasn't the only one that didn't trust Koran.

The sky was quickly darkening and the water in the bay was getting choppy. Clark, Decker and Koran had been talking over assault plans and other military mumbo jumbo, completely ignoring the incoming storm. I tried my best to move them along, but it took an agonizing twenty minutes before they finally agreed on a plan.

"Beer Can Island huh?" Clark asked as we loaded up the black, inflatable motorboat.

"That's the only place they could be or at least where they were an hour ago," Koran replied.

"Well just know, you try anything or if this is some half-baked plan to trick us, I'm gonna bury you and your new friend on that island."

"Of course you will," Koran spat back.

With a nervous fidget, I settled into the boat and grabbed the safety rope. Koran sat down beside me and half-smiled.

"Colonel?" I asked. "The President's daughter?"

"Look, I'm sure it's hard for you to trust me, but there's a lot going on that you don't know about. Let's get our family safe first and if we make it out of this I'll tell you everything."

"My family," I replied. "Half of your family you stole."

Koran frowned then turned toward the back. "We're all set up here."

Clark cranked up the outboard engine and we slowly pulled away from the dock. I could immediately feel the water pushing us around and I wondered if the tiny craft could even make it to the island.

"Hold on," Clark yelled.

Suddenly, the motor growled and the raft cut straight through the waves like a torpedo. We bounced from crest to crest over the whitecaps as the bay turned into a whirlpool. All doubts I had in the boats abilities were erased as we sped over the water toward the island.

My head slammed into the side of the raft and I squeezed the safety rope tighter. Water sprayed my face continuously and the cold wind whipped my eyes into tears.

As the island neared Clark swerved the boat hard to the left and a tub of water splashed over my head. I gasped and wiped my face just as we hit another wave. My feet sailed into the air and I nearly flipped over the bow. Scrambling, I managed to grab hold of the rope before I tumbled into the frigid water.

The boat started to slow and I pulled myself back to the front. The waves continued to knock us around, but I was starting to adjust to it.

"We're gonna pull up around there," Clark pointed. "The three of us will head up the beach, you stay back with the boat."

I wanted to tell Clark to go fuck himself. He'd already gone into great detail about how I'd get everyone killed if I tagged along. Him reiterating the plan now was just to piss me off.

"Yeah, I got it," I replied.

Clark smirked then pulled the boat up to a small enclave. The water pushed and shoved against two giant rocks, creating a little shelter between the jostling waves and the island. A cluster of mangroves shielded us from anyone on shore, their long roots clawing into the sand.

"This is it," Clark said.

He wrapped a rope around one of the rocks then quietly climbed into the water. Decker and Koran followed and I stayed behind like a three-year-old.

"We'll be right back," Koran said and shrugged his shoulders.

That made me even more furious. I didn't even trust Koran and that was my family out there, I needed to be the one saving them.

Stewing, I watched the trio weave between the sprawling mangroves and clamber onto the beach. They quickly vanished and I was left with the sound of the waves as comfort.

Sighing, I sat back on the boat and stared up at the sky. The sun was gone and only oblong, black clouds cluttered the heavens like angry swabs of a paint brush. I'd lost track of time, but I knew it couldn't be that late. We'd only reached the base before day break a few hours ago.

"What's next?" I grumbled to myself.

It felt like hours passed as I waited silently. The wind picked up and started to whip the mangroves around like a baby rattle. The swaying of the raft was like a lullaby and if it hadn't been for my neck breaking anxiety, I would've fallen asleep.

As it was, I stretched out on the bottom of the boat and laid down. My hunger demon was starting to poke out his head and begging me to feed him, but the sea was urging me to empty my stomach into the water. I opted to do both.

Opening my bag, I pulled out the box of crackers we'd found in the store. I ripped open a package and stuffed a handful into my mouth.

At first my stomach thanked me and screamed for more. But as the stale crumbs worked their way down my throat, someone pulled the emergency brake and did a one-eighty.

I lurched over the side of the raft and dry heaved before a stream of water and partially chewed crackers shot forth. I gagged and lapped up a handful of saltwater to clean my mouth. That only made me vomit more and by the time I was done, I was happy to just lay over the side with my face pressed into my hands.

"Come on," a voice suddenly called out.

At first I thought I was delirious and slowly sat up and stared toward the shore.

"Hurry up and get the bucket. I got dibs on the little one and I wanna get back before Timmy spoils her."

I gasped then covered my mouth. Two men were making their way through the mangroves and down toward the water. I scampered over the side of the boat and tried to slide into the chilly tide as quietly as possible.

"Did you hear that?" one of the men asked.

"Hear what?"

"Somebody is down there."

I could hear them picking up speed and I tried to crawl through the water like a crab. My pants felt like anchors and the freezing temperature made me want to find a blanket. But I knew I needed to hide.

I dipped my head under the waves and frog kicked away from the boat. When I came back up the men were nearly in the water, but I'd put enough distance between us that they wouldn't see me immediately.

One of the men was short and fat. He had waterproof overalls on, the kind that fishermen or crabbers wore. His hair was frizzy and white and sprouted out to the side beneath a blue baseball cap. He had a long, white beard and in general, looked like a gnome.

The other man was average height and skinny. His skin looked leathery and sun-worn and his shaggy brown hair fell over his face and covered his eyes. The jeans he wore were ripped up, like he'd been dragged behind a truck and on one foot he had a dirty sneaker and the other a hiking boot.

"What the hell is that?" the short man asked as our boat came into view.

"A damn boat."

"Well shit, I can see it's a boat Dusty. How the hell did it get here?"

"Maybe it's always been here."

I watched the men quietly as they waded closer to the raft. They were suspicious, but more confused than anything else. Their back and forth bickering was almost comical as they argued about the boat.

The skinnier man, Dusty, leaned into the boat and looked around. There was a bag on the floor and some extra jackets that Clark had brought. He rifled through them then rubbed his hand across the side.

"It's still wet," he said then looked in my direction.

My heart exploded from my chest and I jumped in shock. The water splashed and it was just enough for them to notice me.

221

"Frank look!" Dusty shouted and started toward me.

He was quick, much quicker than I thought and before I knew it was only a few yards away, bearing down on me with a rusty knife clutched in his hands. His buddy Frank was still trying to maneuver around the rocks and didn't look too pleased about being in the water.

"You're a dead man!" he shouted at me.

I cringed and tried to scrambled away, but my feet slipped on the rocks. I fell back into the water and the last thing I saw was the blurry image of Dusty leaping toward me, knife first.

CHAPTER 26

WE'RE NOT DEAD YET

Blood poured into the ocean, fading to a thin red as it mixed with the water. Before long, I was surrounded by a crimson pool of it, a halo of death, marking the end of a life that had clocked way too many years already.

I stared through the murky tide as Dusty's face stared defiantly back at me. I could feel his anger and his pain, his deep, brown eyes boring into my soul, screaming with excruciating malice. He leaned closer, then gulped his last breath and the life faded from his face.

I broke the surface in time to see Koran running back toward Frank. He had a small knife in his hands and moved with a sense of murderous purpose.

Before Dusty could reach me, Koran had barreled through the mangroves and buried his knife into Dusty's back. It was a bad way to die, but I was sure he deserved it. Now it was Frank's turn.

To his credit, Frank put up one hell of a fight. Much more than Koran was obviously expecting. He was a scrappy little man.

Before he had a chance to skewer him like Dusty, Frank whipped around and tackled Koran by the waist. They went splashing into the surf and vanished under the tainted water.

When they emerged, Frank had clamped down on Koran's arm like an alligator. He was shaking vigorously while Koran punched him over and over in the head. Frank bit down harder on his knife hand and tried to wrestle the blade away.

With a grunt, Koran grabbed Frank and hoisted him into the air. He slammed him into the water and ripped his arm free. Before Frank could resurface he drove the knife downward with a satisfying yelp. Frank's limbs jerked and snapped momentarily then his body went still.

Huffing, Koran straightened up. He looked around the bay then started toward me. I wiped my face and tried to shake off the feeling of icy death that clung to my skin. Koran grinned then cleaned his knife on his wet jeans.

"We've gotta go," he gasped in an out of breath tone. "Clark and Decker are dead."

"What!" I shouted then covered my mouth with my hands.

"That damn island was crawling with guys, like ten of them. I think we got everyone that spotted us, but those idiots didn't make it. I found where they're keeping the girls. Let's go."

With that, Koran turned around and started heading back toward the beach. I was still in shock from what I'd just heard and my legs refused to obey.

"Randall," he called back to me.

"They...they're dead?"

"If you want to save your family, you don't have time for this shit. Yes, they're dead and if we don't go now your family will be dead too."

Those words got through and I started waddling through the water as fast as I could. I passed Frank's lifeless corpse floating in the shadows and winced. I immediately felt guilty for my weakness. I needed to hate him, I wanted to hate him.

My kids were here. My wife was here. Somehow, he had something to do with it and for that, he deserved worse than death.

I followed Koran onto the shell-ridden beach and through a dense cluster of palms. As we neared the opening, he slowed down then dropped to the ground. I followed his lead and army crawled until we were shoulder to shoulder.

"Up there," he whispered. "Just over that mound there's a shack. The...the girls are inside."

"How do you know?"

"I just know," he said darkly.

"How do we get to it?"

"They had some folk roaming around. They're not here anymore. There's maybe three guys inside. That's it. Stay low and nobody will see us."

Koran pushed himself to his feet and crouched down. He skipped across the sand using his arms like extra legs. He looked like a damn gorilla and in any other situation I would've found it funny, but not today.

I did the same and followed him to a patch of dry grass a few yards from the shack. We took cover there and waited. He wanted to be sure we hadn't been seen. He'd learned the hard way to be careful and Clark and Decker had paid that price with their lives.

"There's a fence around the back," Koran started. "I didn't see that before. We should check it out first."

Before I could reply he'd taken off. He sped around the dense thicket and charged toward the fence. Cursing under my breath, I hurried to catch up. So much for being careful, I thought.

"What the hell?" I asked Koran as I caught up to him.

He didn't reply, his eyes were locked on something up ahead.

"I thought we weren't trying to get killed," I said.

"Look," he replied in a dry voice.

I followed his finger toward the fenced area. At first, I didn't see a thing worth mentioning. Old boat motors, seats from random vehicles and other junk littered the sand. But I continued to look.

"What?" I asked in frustration.

"There!" he said and jabbed his finger toward a pile of junk.

My breath got caught at the back of my tongue and I gagged. Fear and anger swelled inside of me and I almost shouted in rage.

"He's alive," Koran said and placed his hand on my shoulder.

Alistair was laid over in the dirt. His hands had been hogged tied behind his back and his face was bruised and swollen. But like Koran said, he was alive. I could see his chest moving up and down with each breath he took.

"Do you see Charlie and David?" I asked frantically.

"No, but they're probably close. We need to be quick."

Koran held up his knife and pushed it into my hands. Reaching behind his back he pulled out a pistol and checked the magazine.

"I didn't think Clark would need this anymore," he grumbled. "Get your son. I'll keep watch, he probably knows where everyone else is."

I nodded then scampered across the sand toward Alistair. I tried to stay quiet, but I ended up running forward at full speed, my heart thundering with every step I took.

I reached the rusted gate and flung it open. It squealed, but I rushed inside, ignoring the potential danger. Alistair slowly rolled over at the sound and from the look on his face, I was the last person he expected.

"Dad?" he groaned in an almost unfamiliar voice.

I crouched next to him and brushed the sand from his face. "Are you okay?" I asked.

"I'm good. I didn't think you were gonna come."

I laughed. Nothing was funny, not even remotely, but my brain couldn't process real emotions at that moment. Humor was the remedy for the weak.

"I'll never leave you guys," I said. "I'll always be there."

Alistair forced a smile onto his face. Mirroring him, I sawed at the waterlogged, ropes that bound his wrists. Then I cut the ones from around his ankle and helped him to his feet.

He fell into my arms and hugged me. I pulled his head into my shoulder and kissed the top of his head.

"I'm sorry," he groaned and I could feel his tears pouring down my arm.

"Sorry for what?"

"I tried dad, I tried to stop them. I couldn't."

I grabbed him by the shoulders and nudged him back so we were face to face. Wiping the tears from his eyes, I smiled. He was so much better than me. I'd worried about how he would grow up, how strong of a man he'd become. But in that moment, I knew I never needed to worry again.

He bored into me with his soft, brown eyes. I could see the shame and guilt drenched all over his face and it threatened to break me. Alistair was the best of me, he was all that was good in me yet somehow, he thought that wasn't enough.

"Alistair, you have nothing to be sorry for. I'm sorry, I'm sorry I wasn't there when you guys needed me."

"I love you dad," he said.

"I love you too."

I wrapped my arms around him and hugged him again. I held him there, just for a few seconds, but it felt like a lifetime. It felt like he was a little child again and I could hold him there forever. But gone were those days, gone were the times when I could shield him from the dangers of the world. My son had grown up.

I wiped my face and stared around. "Where is everyone?" I asked him.

"They they took mom and Ashley inside," he replied then paused. "David and Charlie are fine," he added as he saw the concern in my face. "They tied them up in a dog crate around the side of the house."

"Take me there."

Koran joined us and we followed Alistair to the far side of the house. Pushed up against the wall was a filthy, blue dog grate. The plastic was frayed and turning brown from dirt and grime and the metal door looked rusted shut.

Charlie and David were crammed inside of it. They were sleeping and had their wrists and feet bound with duct tape. Dirt was smudged to their faces, wet sand caked to their clothes, but they were alive.

A mountain lifted from my chest and I thanked God for my good fortune. Smiling, I moved to open the crate, but Koran grabbed my hand.

"Keep them quiet," he said and pointed at the crust-covered window above.

I nodded and silently started to pry the door open. Charlie moved and I could see that both of their mouths had been covered with duct tape as well and their faces were smeared with dried tears and dirt.

"Shh," I whispered to him as he opened his eyes wide. "You're safe now. I'm gonna take you out of here."

The door creaked and I reached in and grabbed Charlie. His eyes swelled with joy and he shivered. I wiped his face and pulled him into my chest.

"We've got to hurry," Koran urged.

I cut my eyes then kissed Charlie on the head. "Alistair cut the tape," I said and laid Charlie on the ground.

To get David I had to nearly crawl inside of the crate. He was still half asleep and squirmed like a snake as I dragged him into the sand. I could only imagine the horrors they'd been through.

"Stay quiet," I told him. "It's me, it's your dad."

David stared up at me and quivered. There was so much fear in his face and I wanted nothing more than to make it all go away. His eyes started to water and I rubbed the tears away with my fingers.

With him in one arm, I scooped up Charlie and left the fenced yard. I ran around the house and pass the mounds of trash and broken vehicle parts. Alistair followed close behind me, not stopping until we made it back to the mound of dead grass.

There, I laid them down and cut the remaining tape. David jumped up and dove at me. He tried to talk, but his words were swallowed by hyperventilation.

"I love you guys," I said and hugged all three of them.

David started to cry and I squeezed him tighter. I patted the top of his head and let his tears fall onto my neck.

"Did they hurt you?" I asked.

David and Charlie shook their heads from side to side. Alistair made a confirming grunt and I took a deep breath trying to contain my anger.

"Randall!" Koran growled through clenched teeth.

I wanted to turn around and sock him in the side of his head, but he was right. Melinda was still in that shack and God only knew what was being done to her.

"Alistair listen to me," I said as I released them. "Down there, there's a boat. It's tied to the mangroves. I need you to take your brothers and get them on it. Wait there until we come back."

"But dad," he started.

"Listen! I don't have time to argue or explain. I have to get your mom and Ashley and Stephanie."

"Bud dad!"

"Please Alistair. You get down there and you stay quiet. Keep your brothers safe. I love you. I love you guys. Now go!"

I straightened up and turned around. David and Charlie were still sobbing, but I knew Alistair would do what needed to be done. Now, I needed to do what needed to be done.

"Take the gun," Koran said as we headed back toward the shack. "I'm better with the knife than you are."

I stopped and pulled the knife from my belt loop. I handed it to Koran and took his pistol. Swallowing, I clenched my jaw and stared up at the rusty shack with cold eyes.

"Come on," I said and marched forward.

We hurried around the side of the building and knelt at the corner. Scampering on all fours we moved around the front and stopped. There was a window to the left of the door just above our heads.

"I'm gonna check it out," I whispered.

Terrified, I slowly rose my head above the sill and peeked inside. I expected to be greeted with the barrel of a shotgun, but my luck held. It looked like there were only two rooms. The front room was empty and makeshift drapes had been hung in the doorway to separate the backroom from the front.

"It's empty," I said as I crouched back down. "There's another room in the back, we should be able to get inside without anyone seeing us."

Koran nodded and we moved onto the tiny porch up front. The door to the shack was made of thick, unfinished wood. The knob was rusted metal covered in chipped, red paint.

I reached out and grabbed it then looked back to Koran to make sure he was ready. He nodded and I started to mouth the countdown from three.

"Three, two, one," I mumbled before slowly twisting the knob.

CHAPTER 27

WHAT CAN'T BE

BROKEN

I pushed the door open and stepped into the darkness that lay inside. The smell was a dank aroma, like waterlogged clothes and moldy bread. It smacked me in the face like an open hand as soon as I walked through the door.

Up ahead a faint glow cast a hardly noticeable light from the other room. It flickered from the slits between the curtain like a candle or something. A cracked window let in a cool breeze, but the air inside felt moist and dirty.

"You smell that?" Koran whispered.

"Yeah, it fucking reeks."

"No... no. It smells like gasoline or something."

I shrugged and stepped further into the house. A dark brown, wicker chair was tucked into the far corner. A pair of men's jeans and a t-shirt were thrown across it. Other clothes were scattered across the room like someone had undressed in a hurry.

We tried to move silently across the concrete floor. A thin layer of sand shifted with each step we took, but the noises from the other room masked any sound that we did make.

"Hurry up!" an angry, deep voice shouted.

We both froze. I tightened my grip on the pistol and clenched my jaw. Trembling, I looked back to Koran and he nodded his head forward.

"Shut the hell up Timmy. You had plenty of time with the other broad. You ain't save none of that to share," another voice replied.

"Damn it Carl, that's why I let you have the young one first, so we're even."

"Then stop rushing me. This bitch is feisty."

There were at least two men inside and I knew they had the girls with them. I felt a rage come over me. I wanted to rush into the room and shoot everything breathing. But I fought to compose myself and kept edging closer silently.

I stopped right next to the curtains that hung from the ceiling. Koran tapped me on the shoulder and gave me an encouraging nod.

I reached out to grab the purple drapes, but stopped as someone inside grunted.

"I told you be still," the man named Carl shouted angrily.

There was a dull thud and then a whimper. Koran growled and pushed past me. He ripped the curtains down and rushed inside. I followed right behind him, stopping just on the other side of the door.

The room was dim, the only light came from a kerosene lamp that burned dully in the corner. There was a soiled mattress next to it and blankets covering all of the windows.

Ashley was squirming on the edge of the bed. Her mouth had been taped and her face bruised and beaten. A scrawny, grungy old man was pressed in between her legs. His long, gray hair was knotted together and fell down his back. He had sparse patches of facial hair and tattoos up and down his arms. His skin was tanned and leathery like he'd spent a lifetime in the outdoors, like the sun and the spray of saltwater were home to him.

Ashley was doing her best to resist him. He was pushing and pulling at her legs, trying to thrust his naked body in between them. Every time he grabbed one of her legs, she'd kick out the other one, pushing him away. She earned several blows to the face for her efforts, but she didn't quit fighting.

The man named Carl froze when he saw us. His eyes grew like balloons and some barbaric grunt got stuck in his throat.

Koran didn't waste any time. He took three strides and was on Carl in seconds. Koran's knife slid into the small of his back as he grabbed Carl's hair and yanked his head backward.

"Argh!" Carl shouted.

Koran snatched the knife out and blood sprayed onto the floor. With a quick jab, he buried the blade into the base of the Carl's neck. Carl gasped and his arms snapped wildly like a dying spider. He let out a garbled breath then his muffled groans fell silent.

Koran released his hair and stepped to the side as Carl toppled backward. Blood streamed down his bare chest and his eyes flickered like dying butterfly wings.

Ashley ripped the tape from her mouth and screeched. Jumping to her feet, she stomped on him over and over as she punctuated each blow with a howl of pain.

There was another man to my left, Timmy. He'd been undressing when we walked in and was caught with his foot halfway out of one of his pants legs. He reached for a gun that was sitting on the far nightstand, but he tripped over his dingy jeans and landed on all fours.

Without a single feeling of remorse, I raised the pistol and fired three shots into his face. Blood and brains peppered the wall behind him and Timmy collapsed to the. Smoke swirled from the barrel of my gun and my ears rung in pain, but I'd never felt so powerful in my life.

Something moved out of the corner of my eye and I whipped around. Melinda stared at me with blank eyes and I dropped the gun

236

and rushed toward her. She wrapped her hands around my neck and I scooped her into my arms.

"Are you okay? Did they touch you? Did they hurt you?" I rattled off.

She didn't immediately answer. She stared me in the face then burst into tears. I squeezed her and ran my hand over her head. She collapsed into my embrace and I felt a pain in my heart like someone was crushing it with pliers.

"I'm fine...I'm fine she sobbed, but."

"Where's Stephanie?" Koran asked as he spun in place.

I looked around the room in confusion. Stephanie was nowhere to be seen. Koran had wrapped Ashley with a sheet and sat her onto the bed. Melinda was squeezing me like a lifeline, but Stephanie...I hadn't seen her.

"Randall," Melinda sobbed. "Randall listen."

"Where is Stephanie?" Koran said again in a deeper tone. "Stephanie!"

"Randall!" Melinda exclaimed and grabbed me by the shoulders.

I looked down at her and she pointed to a shadowy doorway near the back. We'd missed it when we first came in, but there was something ominous and malevolent that seemed to spew from the dark.

"The restroom," she said lowly.

"Wait here," I told her.

I raised my gun and called out to Koran. I motioned toward the doorway and he tightened the grip on his knife and marched toward it.

"Stephanie," he called again. "Stephanie, are you in there."

I followed behind him and leaned against the wall next to the door. I was ready, ready for whatever evil hid just out of sight.

Reaching into the darkness, Koran felt on the wall for a light switch. His fingers found it and as the light illuminated the bathroom I watched all of the life fade from Koran's face.

"No!" he roared.

CHAPTER 28

WHAT WILL BE BROKEN

The scene was horrific. Blood was splattered everywhere. The grimy walls were stained with the crimson traces of death. The mirror bore streaks from fingers covered in blood and a cracked smear from where someone's face had impacted it.

The towel rack had been torn from the wall and the dirty toilet had a fracture running down the side. Everything about the bathroom was wrong, everything was tainted with pain and death.

I edged inside and passed Koran. The bathroom was long and narrow and ended with a dirt smudged bath tub. Inside of it was a shower curtain with dark green floral patterns and peacocks. It was covering something, something that Koran couldn't bear to reveal himself, but I knew it needed to be done.

I walked toward the tub and knelt down. With shaky hands, I reached out and grabbed the curtain. I took a deep breath and pulled it back.

"Fuck!" I cringed.

Crumpled in the tub was Stephanie's broken body. She was naked and covered from head to toe in welts and bruises. Her face was eternally frozen in the painful grimace she died in, but her bruised knuckles showed that she hadn't gone quietly.

I turned to face Koran and his eyes dulled over. He'd completely lost it. He groaned in pain and fell to the floor, before crawling across the tile to the bath tub.

"Stephanie no," he crooned in a voice that made my bones ache.

He reached out and grabbed her hand. Tears poured from his eyes and fell onto her face, leaving streaks in the layers of blood.

"I'm so sorry...I'm so, so sorry," Koran croaked.

I stood up and backed away. I didn't have the words to comfort him and I felt like me being there was intruding on something private that no one should be a witness to.

"Randall!" Melinda suddenly called.

I turned around and saw the trail of smoke before she said another word. The lamp had fallen over and caught fire to one of the blankets that covered the window. The tiny room had suddenly erupted into a raging inferno.

"Koran!" I shouted as I rushed and grabbed Melinda. "Koran!"

Ashley had moved from the bed and was starting toward the other room. I ripped the curtain down and walked them both to the front door.

"I'll get Koran, wait here," I told them.

The flames were spreading quickly. They'd already burned the curtains and started to melt the windows. A loud crackle exploded as the glass popped and the fire roared up.

Black smoke was everywhere. I fanned my way toward the bathroom nearly blind. The heat felt like it was going to melt my skin and the creaking frame of the shack threatened to collapse at any second.

"Koran!" I screamed.

He was still sitting at the edge of the tub. He had Stephanie's bloody, hand pressed against his face. His lips were quivering as he mumbled incoherently under his breath.

"Koran," I called again in a softer voice.

I edged my way closer to him, coughing as the smoke grew thicker. Timidly, I reached out and touched his shoulder. He jumped and spun around with bloodshot eyes.

"Koran, we have to go."

"No... no. She's sleeping, she'll get up soon."

I swallowed and took a deep breath. "She's not sleep. Look, there's a fire, we have to get out of here now," I told him as calmly as I could.

"Just leave me here. I'll bring her with me when she wakes up."

There was a loud bang in the other room as a beam fell from the ceiling. Melinda screamed my name as ash and cinders floated into the air.

"Koran!" I shouted.

Grabbing his arm, I pulled him away. He yelled and fought against me, but he couldn't get traction on the filthy floor. I literally dragged him kicking and screaming.

"Let me go! Get off of me damn it!" he snapped.

I managed to pull him into the other room where the fire was rolling across the ceiling. It moved like it had a mind of its own, like it was a thinking creature, setting a trap. The threat of mortal danger seemed to bring some sense into Koran and he awkwardly shuffled to his feet.

"I can't leave her Randall. I can't leave her," he said to me.

Another beam collapsed and the flames shot up like fireworks. The walls rattled and the rickety shack croaked like it was dying. I frowned and grabbed Koran's arm.

"We have to go. There's nothing we can do. We're all gonna die in here."

He stared back into the bathroom and wiped his face. Mumbling, he winced and started to cry some more as the flames flared engulfed the doorway to the bathroom. I pulled his arm and he reluctantly followed, but he was broken.

We rushed into the first room and bolted outside with Ashley and Melinda. The fresh air was reviving, but the storm clouds had swooped in with a vengeance. We'd traded one disaster for another.

"Where are the kids? Did you find the kids Randall?" Melinda asked.

"They're waiting on the boat, they're okay. We need to go."

Koran took a deep breath and straightened up. He held out a pair of jeans and a t-shirt to Ashley. "I... I, I found...found you these," he stuttered.

"Thanks," Ashley whispered with a faint smile.

We turned our backs as she got dressed then started toward the water. The wind was whipping blasts of sand into our faces, but we moved quick and purposefully.

"Mom!" I could hear the boys' voices in unison as we cleared the mangroves.

They shouted and cried out to her, nearly capsizing the boat. Alistair jumped out to help and grabbed his mom by the arm. She hugged him and kissed his cheek.

"Alistair, I told you to stay in the boat," I snapped.

"Dad I'm fine."

Holding onto Alistair's arm, Melinda climbed inside and grabbed Charlie and David. "Are you guys okay? They didn't hurt you, did they? God I missed you, I was so scared," she rattled.

Wrapping their hands around her, they cried and smothered her with kisses. I watched them silently, thanking God that we were back together. I couldn't imagine my life without them.

Alistair turned and went to help Koran with Ashley. As soon as she saw him she fell into his arms and burst into tears. He hugged her back and gave her a kiss on the cheek.

"You...you gonna be alright?" he asked. "What happened?"

"I'm okay. I just want to get out of here."

Ashley held his arm as she cautiously stepped down the rocks. Wincing, she crawled into the raft and crouched into a ball. Alistair frowned then went back up toward the beach to grab the blanket she dropped.

The waves in the bay started to pick up and were pushing the raft from side to side. I grabbed the front of the boat then looked back for Alistair. He was standing beside Koran with his hands on his hips, looking out over the water. Koran was mumbling something to him, while he balanced on the rocks.

"Let's move," I called to them. "The storm is getting close."

I was really worried about Koran. He'd just lost his wife and I couldn't begin to think how that was going to affect him. Right now, he was in shock. He was operating without really being there and to anyone that didn't know, he seemed normal. But that was going to end soon and I didn't know him well enough to even guess what the long-term damage would be.

Just as I started to call to them again, something moved from behind the mangroves. I jumped at the sound and stared in shock. A fear gripped me like claws on the back of my neck and my voice turned to a whisper.

A shirtless man with greasy, black hair stormed toward the beach. He had a rifle in his hand and the look of menace on his face.

As he rounded the corner and shouldered his gun, I screamed at the top of my lungs in vain. Reaching into my waistband, I pulled out the pistol Koran had given me, but his gun rang out before I could even level mine.

It felt like it took a lifetime for the bullet to find it's mark. In retaliation, I unleashed two shots from my own pistol and roared in anger. I stared helplessly from the water, unable to hold onto a single thought or action.

In slow motion, Alistair jolted forward. He collapsed into the murky froth, just as my bullets tore into the man. Watching Alistair fall was like seeing myself get shot through someone else's eyes. I felt the pain as if the searing metal had pierced my own flesh.

"Alistair no!" I screamed.

CHAPTER 29

WHATEVER TOMORROW BRINGS

The boat bounced up and down across the jolting waves. I held Alistair's head in my hands as if I could protect him from the turbulent ride, as if I could protect him from what had already been done. As if I could protect him at all.

The idea, the thought was simply ironic. I'd failed at protecting him in so many ways and now I pit my will against gravity. What could one man do, when it seemed like fate itself had turned against you?

Alistair was laying across the bottom of the boat, a bullet lodged in his hip, death nipping at his heels. His skin was cold and pale from the loss of blood and the time he spent in the icy water, meant almost certain hypothermia.

"Keep fighting Alistair, keep fighting," I whispered to him.

Melinda had finally stopped crying. Now she simply held his hands and shivered in fear. David and Charlie looked on with confused guises. They were old enough to know that something was wrong and young enough for that idea to terrorize them.

"We're close," Koran called up to us as he maneuvered the motor.

Across the choppy, gray water I could see the mangled dock. Two of Clark's men, Hunter and Shipley were standing on it, staring out at us. More soldiers were rushing down the walkway from the office buildings. I was sure they'd been expecting our return for some time. Clark had pitched this as some easy, *over in a jiffy mission*, but he was so very, very wrong.

"Dad," Alistair groaned. "Dad I'm cold."

I'd already covered him with my jacket and tried to push the sides up under him to keep out the wind. The fact that he was soaking wet didn't really help, but there wasn't much else I could do besides hug him and pray.

"We're almost there," I replied.

"I'm scared dad. I don't want to die."

"You're not gonna die. I promise, I promise you'll be fine."

Melinda started crying again and I clenched my jaw, holding back the tidal wave of pain that I felt. I was helpless and I needed to do something, anything, to bring some kind of control back to the situation.

The drone from the boat motor echoed out across the water. It whined as we collided with the massive waves and sailed into the air. Suddenly, there was another sound, much louder and deeper.

"What the hell was that?" Koran boomed.

A ripple ran across the surface of the water as it churned wildly. Ahead of us a massive wave rose into the air. Koran swerved the boat to avoid it and I nearly fell into the ocean. With a thundering boom, the water crashed, pushing the raft onto its side.

Behind us, the island we'd just left cracked in half. Water rushed down the middle of it as chunks plunged under the frothing waves. It was like the Earth was swallowing itself.

"Get us to the pier!" I shouted.

The bay swirled around us, pushing and slapping the boat from side to side. Koran tried his best to steer us clear of the largest waves and angled toward the boardwalk. Hunter and Shipley were screaming and waving their hands, but we couldn't hear them over the roar of the wind and water.

The sound of a raging jackhammer cracked the air above us. I looked up as two enormous helicopters with props on either side floated toward the base. It was like I was watching a movie, there was no way this reality played a part in my life.

Howling wind blew whitecaps out in the distance. Screeches and deep thuds echoed as the ground ripped apart. The boat zipped through the raging storm as two giant, leaf-colored helicopters slowly lowered into a field behind the marina.

"Hang on!" Koran screamed.

With a clunk, we slid into the dock. The swelling water nearly pushed us onto the planks and the spinning props hacked into the crumbling wood before Koran could shut off the engine.

"We gotta go now!" Hunter snapped.

The rickety dock trembled as the water slammed into it. I quickly helped Ashley and the kids up and Shipley rushed them from the dock onto solid ground. Melinda climbed off of the boat behind them then turned back to me.

"Hurry Randall," she said.

Hunter stopped Ashley and looked her over. "You okay miss?" he asked over the loud whooshing noise.

"I'm fine," Ashley said dismissively.

I grabbed Alistair and with Koran's help I pulled him onto the dock. He groaned in pain and it broke my heart to see him in such misery. All I could do was pray that we'd make it in time.

"We need a stretcher and a doctor," I yelled out.

"What happened to him?" Hunter asked.

"He got shot. We need a fucking doctor now!"

"Lockship! Get over here!" Hunter yelled.

249

Kneeling down, he swung his bag off of his shoulders and started unfolding what looked like a lawn chair. Within seconds it morphed into a stretcher and we were loading Alistair onto it and carrying him into the field.

"What happened?" Lockship asked as he stopped alongside us.

"He got shot," I replied angrily.

"Put him down...put him down here," Lockship ordered.

We lowered Alistair onto the ground and Lockship started doing whatever it was medical professionals did. He had his little medical kit and some kind of device that he clipped onto Alistair's index finger.

"How you feeling buddy," Lockship asked.

Alistair bellowed like a pissed off mule as Lockship turned him onto his side. Melinda looked concerned, but I considered any sounds he made a good sign. Lockship smiled and patted his arm.

"Where's Clark and Decker?" Hunter asked as he caught up.

"They didn't make it," Koran replied.

Hunter gave him a look, but didn't push any further. "We've gotta get out of here now!"

To punctuate that notion the ground trembled and the remaining pieces of the dock fell into the bay. Water splashed up against the seawall and started to flood the surrounding lawn. I could hardly believe what I was seeing, the ocean was drinking the world away.

"Help me get him on the bird," Lockship suddenly said. "Come on!"

"Is he gonna be okay?" Melinda asked as she cradled David and Charlie in her arms.

Ashley stood behind her, looking on with watery eyes. She hadn't said much, but I could tell she was terrified of losing him.

"Doesn't look like the bullet hit anything major. He's stable now, but not out of the woods, but we need to get him to a trauma center, I can't do anything with him here."

Hunter looked at all of us and chewed the inside of his jaw. His eyes rested on Ashley then back to Koran. Then he glanced over to the water that was decidedly working its way further and further inland. "Let's go," he said. "Everybody on the helicopter."

The other soldiers ushered us toward the aircraft. The swirling blades blew dirt and debris into the air, but we pushed past it. Running up the ramp, we loaded Alistair into the closest chopper then buckled up the kids. More soldiers piled into the other helicopter as the water worked its way closer and closer.

Hunter and his men loaded in with us. Trampling onto the helicopter, they buckled into the seats and laid their rifled across their laps. Lockship stayed right beside Alistair the entire time. I was grateful to have him there.

"Hunter," Koran said as he stopped and grabbed him by the arm. "I brought her," he started. "Just like I said I would. She's here."

"Okay?" Hunter replied.

"So, don't forget what we talked about."

"Yeah, yeah...I understand."

Water splashed against the skids and Hunter glanced back outside. Everything was going to shit. The wind was picking up and the bay was spooling up like a blender.

I could read the worry on Hunter's face and I was sure it was the same as mine. We'd survived so much and still, we weren't out of the woods yet. Clenching his jaw, Hunter took a deep breath then motioned up toward the pilot.

"Get these things in the air!" he shouted.

Lockship started an IV on Alistair. I pulled Melinda and the kids in close and prayed under my breath. The weather was damn near torrential and the ground was falling apart beneath us. It seemed like there was no place that was safe.

I felt my stomach turn as the engines grew louder. With a shimmy, the rotors spun up and the molded chunk of metal left the ground.

"Dad are we flying?" Charlie asked.

"We sure are," I replied. "You're not scared, are you?"

"Not anymore."

"Well, that makes one of us," I said with a laugh.

The helicopter shuddered from side to side as we climbed higher into the air. The wind seemed intent on stopping us, but the thundering rotors hacked right through it as we left the base and headed into the unknown.

Ashley leaned out of her seat and grabbed Alistair's hand. She interlaced her fingers with his and squeezed. "You'll be okay," she whispered.

Alistair smiled and placed his other hand over hers. He pulled it to his chest and took a deep breath.

I think if they could, they would've stayed like that forever. There was something about going through tragedy together. The immediacy of it all made emotions much more potent. It was strange to watch and heartbreaking to know that such things seldom lasted.

"Hey," Koran called out to Hunter.

"Yeah?"

"Mayflower," he said. "You promised...you would take us to Mayflower."

Hunter glared at him. He clenched his jaw and ground his teeth together. Sighing, he turned and looked toward the back of the helicopter then reluctantly nodded.

"What's Mayflower?" Melinda asked.

~THE END~

~Continue the journey with~

"The Mayflower Project: Deconstruction Book Two"

Buy Now!!

Click here to join the mailing list for updates, access to special features, new releases and the monthly newsletter.

Continue reading for a sneak peek at The Mayflower Project:

Deconstruction Book Two

Sneak Peek...The Mayflower Project

CHAPTER 1

THE COUNTDOWN CLOCK

"Max, are you gonna finish that," Suzanne asked me.

I looked up at her and sighed. Of course, I was gonna finish that. There were maybe three bites left of my ham and cheese sandwich and I was holding the damn thing in my hand. But the way she was staring at me, I feared she might snatch it and run off.

"Where does all of the food you eat even go?" I asked and narrowed my eyes.

Suzanne was a tall, light-skinned lady from some island in the Caribbean. She apparently worked out like a track athlete, although I had no proof, other than her physique and the fact that she ate like a linebacker, but managed to never gain a pound.

She smiled at me and grabbed the remainder of my sandwich. "Thanks Max. You're a keeper."

"I was gonna eat that," I screamed after her.

Sighing, I got up and cleaned off the table then left the break room. I walked down the hall and back into the work area at the National Weather Service Center in Georgia. You had to say it that way or no one would understand you. People didn't understand what we did anyway, but avoiding acronyms or any shortening of the name, made me feel like I'd chosen the right path in school.

Around the office, we spoke in a short code on just about everything. NOAA, EPA, SAB, E3, E&C, NAI, SCAN, SDR...the list went on. It was enough to give anyone a headache. So, when I had the opportunity, I spoke like a normal person.

Lately, the list of names in the office had become much more ominous and terms like CIA, NSA, DIA and NORAD were getting thrown around. All of our work had become compartmentalized and guys with dark suits and strong, jaw bones lurked in every corner.

All of this additional security made me nervous and as far as anyone outside of work was concerned, all I did was track hurricanes and send alerts to the surrounding Emergency Operations Centers. But that couldn't be further from the truth.

I was a climatologist, a damn good one. Science had always been my thing and luckily it worked out. At the ripe young age of twenty-seven I'd managed to snag a senior position working with the government. A position that I still couldn't believe I had.

It all started with a paper I'd written back in school. It was a soapbox moment, but after getting passed around a few times the paper garnered some serious attention.

It was about thermodynamics and climate change and a theory I proposed, called the "Neilman Effect"...my last name. Basically, the Earth was dying. I suggested we'd be faced with cataclysmic disaster on a global scale in this lifetime. The report was interlaced with a healthy bit of speculative fiction, but someone important read it and decided it sounded a little too probable to ignore.

 So, here I was, heading up a secret team in an inconspicuous building. Plotting charts, making graphs and giving predictions that set the ground floor for policy. All because someone had read my dissertation and concluded that Max Neilman could save the world.

"Max, you get the reports over to the DOD? They need the update before the last mailing goes out," Bruce asked.

He was an older man with silvery hair and thick, eyebrows. He needed glasses, but he seldom wore them and he liked to part his hair right down the middle and chew the end of any pen he could get his hands on.

"Yeah Bruce, I sent them." I stopped and looked up at the giant, digital clock that took up the wall.

The idea that you needed a clock the size of a movie screen was a clear indication of how serious things were, but if the message still wasn't received, the bright, red numbers that ticked away slowly, would've hammered home the sense of peril. It read **987 Days: 14**

Hours: 17:26, an arbitrary time frame, but people needed something to shoot for.

As the numbers vanished I cringed and ground my teeth. Time, man's greatest invention. It was the only way we could comprehend our place in the universe and it was the only way we could even attempt to acknowledge our mortality. But it was an invention nonetheless, a nonsensical representation that made us feel better. A way that we could convince ourselves that things didn't just happen.

"Staring at it is not gonna make it go back up," Bruce snapped.

"Yeah, I know. It's just...maybe, maybe we got it wrong."

"Err on the side of caution Max. You did good here."

I took a deep breath and held it. That was just it, maybe I hadn't been cautious enough. Everything had been extrapolated from my research. Everything had been built around something I'd written while intoxicated and under insane stress.

Sure, my work had been second guessed and scrutinized by probably hundreds of other scientists. Sure, experts had weighed in and tried to tear my research apart, but no one knew the data like me. If the estimates were wrong, that was my fault.

Bruce stepped closer to me and leaned in. "Mayflower is your baby. No one might ever tell you and only a handful of people will even know what you did, but all of this is because of you."

"Thanks Bruce," I said and patted him on the shoulder.

Mayflower, that name was seldom spoken. As far as code names went, it was probably the most secretive of all. Only a few even knew of its existence and an even smaller group understood the details in their entirety. I was part of that group.

"Look sharp, we have visitors today." With that Bruce headed back to his desk.

Rubbing my face, I walked back to my office and closed the door. I plopped into my chair and let my head fall forward onto the solid oak. I counted to twenty then sat up and stared at the wall.

There was a map taped to the cream painted brick. It was zoomed in on the mid-western United States and had pins stuck in places all over Wyoming. I'd recommended Colorado, but decisions like that weren't really left up to me.

So, somewhere up in the Rocky Mountains there was a secret. The government had its tentacles at work and had set the many segments of this powerful nation to task, without one arm knowing what the other one was doing.

That was the Mayflower. That was the secret that many had already taken to their grave. That was why I was under constant surveillance, like everyone else that worked down there and that was why every night, I went home and lied to my girlfriend.

"I just need more time," I mumbled to myself.

I picked up a picture frame, looked at it and smiled. Cindy smiled back at me and I thought about life before all of this. I thought about my life when I was just Max and no one expected anything else from me.

Mediocrity had its pluses and being in this place made you miss them. What I missed most though was being invisible. It wasn't like I was famous or anything, but within a small circle everyone knew who I was and watched everything I did. The guy in that photo never had to worry about things like that.

We'd taken the picture during a trip to North Carolina. We'd visited a place called slippery rock and spent the rest of the week hiking through the mountains. It was one of the best times of my life and the first time I looked at Cindy as someone I could get old with.

Now, we never had time for anything. Cindy lived with her nose in a book, studying to take the bar. And I was always here, doing things I couldn't even tell her about. Most days we hardly saw each other and when we did it was for a few minutes before we both fell asleep.

"Max," I heard Bruce call as he tapped on the door.

"Come on in," I replied.

The door swung open and Bruce was standing outside with two more men. They both were wearing navy blue suits and were probably in their late sixties. I recognized one of the men and felt my throat tighten just a bit.

"Hello Secretary Morris," I said with a smile.

"Max," he replied and stepped inside. "This is Timothy Garner, Secretary of Defense. Why don't you go ahead and tell us about the Mayflower?"

CHAPTER 2

PARTY AT THE END OF THE WORLD

I got home around seven and headed up the elevator to my Atlanta apartment. The commute from Peachtree was about an hour and I usually spent that time second guessing everything I'd done earlier. We lived right in the heart of the financial district, which was good for Cindy since she worked there, but meant crappy traffic for me just about every day.

"You home?" I asked as I walked inside and dropped my bags.

"In the bedroom," Cindy replied.

I made my way through the living room and she walked out. Cindy was a tall, athletically built former track star at Georgia Tech.

She could still outrun my ass in her sleep and since she was nearly my height I tried to ban heels whenever I could.

Her father was from South Africa and her mother Honduras. The combination was what I thought every woman should look like. Perfect skin, perfect hair and a full command of five languages while I struggled with two. I knew it, so it didn't bother me when people would say how lucky I was. I'd rather be lucky than good looking any day of the week.

"How was work?" she asked.

I collapsed onto our sofa and tapped the spot to my right. She joined me and leaned into my shoulder while I stroked her hair.

"It was long," I finally replied. "But you know...just another day at the office."

Cindy smiled. "I know the feeling. We need a vacation."

"Now you're talking."

"I'm serious, I have another month before I take the bar. We should go somewhere. I'm sure I can get away from the office for a week...and a break from studying would probably be good for me."

"It would be nice to do something different. I'm just not sure if I can get time off right now."

"Max!" someone yelled as the doorbell rang.

Cindy groaned and I let out a laugh.

"You asked for something different," I said and headed to the door.

I opened it and Brent and Jake stormed inside. They rushed past me and made a beeline for the couch. Cindy barely had time to slide over as they dove onto it and made themselves at home.

"We got a plan guys," Jake said in excitement.

"No...no, we are not going out," I replied and held my hands up in a pleading manner.

Brent and Jake lived next door. We'd known them for about five years and they were still living like we were freshmen in college. Only difference was they had the money of a blossoming start-up to fund their alcohol-driven weekends.

"Just listen to me Max," Jake said. He was the salesman of the two. Tall, dark-skinned and baldheaded, he looked like a wanna be Michael Jordan. He was a pretty funny guy and had absolutely no athletic ability whatsoever, but his charisma went a long way. He could talk himself out of just about anything.

"Yeah," Brent added. "Listen to him."

Brent was the brains of the operation. An average sized guy with stringy, brown hair and glasses. He'd been a coder since he was like twelve and with Jake's inspiration had created some trading algorithm that helped brokers make more money, as if they needed that. When we first met him, he was pretty uptight, but nowadays Jake's influence was starting to rub off.

"Alright Jake, what is this plan you have?" I asked.

"Prive is having a giant event tonight. It's DJ Cosmo's launch party. We have to go! We get in there, get some drinks and get crazy!"

"This is your big plan?" Cindy sighed and rolled her eyes.

"Brent got us VIP."

"You know I hate clubs," I said with disdain and kicked my feet up onto the coffee table.

"Dude come on. It's Friday, you guys never do shit anymore. Remember how it used to be? We were like the three musketeers."

"There's four of us."

"Yeah, but Cindy is a chick."

"Hey!" Cindy objected.

"He means, you're like the fair princess that we have to protect," Brent added.

"Yeah, that's exactly what I meant. So come on Max. What do you say? It's VIP...open bar dude."

Cindy nudged me with her elbow. I turned and she raised her eyebrows and gave me an encouraging shrug.

"Really?" I asked in shock.

"Really!" she replied.

The next thing I knew I was in a noisy nightclub with blinding strobe lights, burning my retinas. I could feel the bass vibrating my chest cavity and the multiple shots of vodka were doing nothing to dull my senses.

The place was packed and whoever this DJ was, he had a lot of friends. I was amazed so many people could fit in one building and if it wasn't for Brent getting VIP we wouldn't have had a place to sit.

"Come on," Cindy said.

She grabbed my arm and pulled me to the dance floor. For the next twenty minutes I reluctantly bobbed around with a crowd full of sweaty people, while Cindy pretended I was a stripper pole.

It was hard to enjoy myself when I had so much on my mind. I really didn't like nightclubs to begin with and now with all that was going on at work, it just felt like more stress that I didn't need. But I was a good sport, so I danced and danced until Cindy told me her feet hurt and she wanted to sit down.

After that it was back to our VIP booth and more shots until I couldn't see straight. Jake and Brent were doing their best to make me permanently stupid and on some level, they certainly succeeded.

"Enough of this vodka shit," I slurred. "Where's the Patron?"

"Patron?" Jake echoed. "You sure about that?"

"Don't you ask me stupid questions. I said Patron Goddamn it."

Laughing, Jake flagged down our server and soon enough the fiery taste of death was burning its way through my digestive system. Like a toddler, I slid off of the sofa and flopped onto the floor in a laughing fit. Everything was suddenly hilarious and I felt like dancing was the only cure.

Pushing myself onto my knees, I grabbed Cindy around the waist. "Come on...more dancing," I grumbled.

She stared at me with glossy eyes then mumbled something I couldn't make out. I started to protest, but then I felt the urge to empty my stomach and I threw my hand over my mouth.

I quickly jumped to my feet and rushed off to the restroom. Bursting through the door, I dove into the first stall and lurched forward. A stream of vomit came spewing out as my knees buckled and I dropped to the floor.

The toilet was filthy. Stains and puddles of piss were everywhere. But at that point I didn't care. I wrapped my arms around the bowl and heaved forward.

"Hey man, you okay in there?" Brent called from the door.

"Argh! Okay!" I shouted back then collapsed face first onto the toilet seat.

"Alright man...I'll leave you to it."

He closed the door and left. It took me thirty minutes longer to puke out enough to regain some of my senses. I could barely stand afterward, but I was pretty sure I'd just survived alcohol poisoning.

Feeling like shit, I shuffled to the sink and doused my head with water. I goggled and spit and washed my face over and over. The taste of vomit still lingered regardless. It was like my taste buds had been permanently damaged.

I leaned my head back then felt the floor shift a bit under my feet and the mirror trembled. I shook my head from side to side and blinked wildly then slapped myself in the face. I definitely had too much to drink.

"Get your shit together," I said as I stared into the mirror.

I smacked myself a few more times and took some deep breaths. Clenching my fists, I screamed at the top of my lungs. My head was still spinning, but the sting on my cheek told me I was awake.

Feeling a bit more like myself, I headed out of the bathroom. A cluster of women were standing in the hall and giggled as I stumbled by. Some loud trance music was playing and the bass was shaking the walls like a damn speaker grill.

I staggered my way back to the VIP section. Cindy was slumped over on Jake's shoulder and Brent was twirling around with some blonde chick that was swigging Vodka from the bottle.

"He's alive," Brent announced as I got closer. "We got bottles to kill before we leave here."

He grabbed the bottle from his dance partner and held it out to me. I reached for it, but suddenly the floor jutted up and I fell into the wall. The bottle slipped from his hands and burst into millions of tiny glass missiles.

I straightened up and looked around. Everyone else was glaring in confusion as well. A few people had fallen, others had spilled drinks or knocked over bottles on the bar. This time I wasn't imagining, something was going on.

"What the hell was that? Brent asked as he chuckled and wrapped his arm around the blonde chick's waist. "Who cares," he continued. "Let's party!"

Suddenly, the ground moved again and a loud rumble echoed over the music. With a crash, a crack split right down the middle of the ceiling and down the dance floor like a mirror image. The shelves behind the bar toppled over and gallons of top-shelf liquor spread across the ground like a tidal wave.

The floor rolled up and down. Fissures split open across the tile and the building shook so violently I thought a train was passing on top of us. The rattling walls made it impossible for me to even think straight and I stood in place like they say possums do when they see headlights.

The sounds of screams pushed me further into a state of drunken panic. Chunks of plaster and cement collided with human flesh, silencing forever those not quick enough to move. Metal beams snapped from the ceiling and showered the floor like arrows. Chaos spiraled all around me and I was too dazed to react until I heard someone shouting.

"Earthquake!"

<u>Read the full version</u>

Follow me on Twitter: @RashadFreeman

www.rashadfreeman.com

–

–

DECONSTRUCTION THE SERIES

Loved it, liked it or hated it?

I'd love to hear your feedback; please leave a review.

About the Author

The date was October 31, 1979. The air was cool and a light fog blew in from the gulf, cloaking the Tampa area in an ominous, tight-fitting tunic. The annual Halloween festivities had just begun and a night of mischievous tomfoolery was afoot.

Scandalous and nefarious characters took flight. Doorbells were rung and ill-boding tricks were played regardless of the treats given. This was the dark reality of the bustling Florida metropolitan.
To the north, Grateful Dead crooned the night's theme music at the Nassau Coliseum. Within earshot of the concert, witnesses stated a UFO hovered over the grounds for thirty minutes before vanishing.
At the same time the Cromarty's were busy hosting their notorious Halloween party at 112 Ocean Ave., better known as the Amityville Horror House. Screams and cries for help were reported throughout the night, punctuated with the disappearance of the family next door.
They were never heard from again.
Unknowingly altering the course of history, Kurt Vonnegut released "Jailbird" the same week KISS gained infamy on The Tomorrow Show. The aftermath of this collision would not be felt for decades until the emergence of Justin Bieber.
After a night filled with mayhem and destruction and the deaths of several prominent entertainers, politicians and a notorious bank robber, the Federal government was forced to loan $1.5 billion dollars to Chrysler. This spurred a series of violent protests, resulting in the Brunah Agate oil spill. Over 10.7 million gallons of oil were

dumped into the Galveston Bay. This became the worst oil spill disaster in U.S. history.
A few hours later, on November 1, 1979, Rashad Freeman was born. Feel free to draw your own conclusions.

"I'm a writer, I right things."

Follow Rashad and stay updated on the series and other books @

http://www.rashadfreeman.com

Other titles you might like

Printed in Great Britain
by Amazon